D0359976

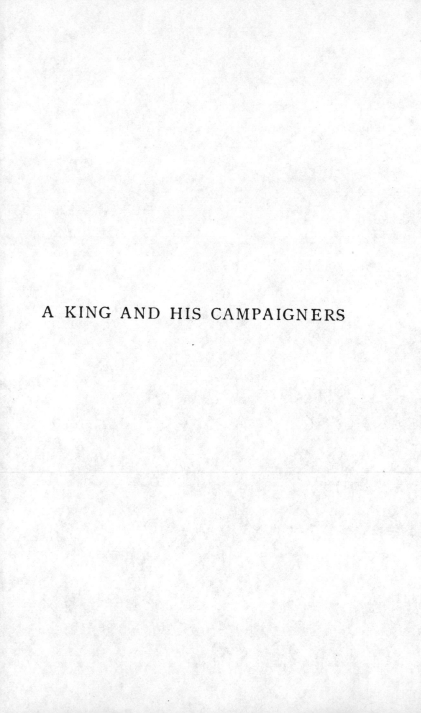

A KING AND HIS CAMPAIGNERS

VERNER VON HEIDENSTAM

A KING AND HIS CAMPAIGNERS

Rendered into English by

AXEL TEGNIER

Short Story Index Reprint Series

BOOKS FOR LIBRARIES PRESS
FREEPORT, NEW YORK

First Published 1902
Reprinted 1970

STANDARD BOOK NUMBER:
8369-3405-9

LIBRARY OF CONGRESS CATALOG CARD NUMBER:
70-113676

PRINTED IN THE UNITED STATES OF AMERICA

CONTENTS.

TRANSLATOR'S NOTE.

VERNER VON HEIDENSTAM, a great Little Master in
latter-day Swedish literature, is in his narrative style
inclined towards impressionism. The very simplicity
of his style, its bald directness of effect, his suggestion
of environment and character by means of scanty but
illuminating detail, and the veiledness of his root in-
tention, make the effort to render his writings into
proper English invidious and hard to achieve with
any just measure of success.

The stories in this volume, the first of the series
entitled " Karolinerna " in the Swedish, deal with the
condition of the country and the personality of
Charles XII., that military genius of the early part
of the eighteenth century. At the age of eighteen
he smote Russia, Denmark, and Saxony with her
Polish sovereign, who were conspiring to partition
his kingdom; and to him Marlborough could say,
"I wish I could serve in some campaign under so
great a general as your Majesty, that I might learn
what I yet want to know."

Heidenstam's work, vivid and picturesque, is
charged with a deep knowledge of the period treated.
Local colour is dealt out with a sparing hand; only
here and there a patch of it lightens the monotone of

his general scheme; and superfluous detail is rigorously eschewed. His delineation of Charles, that ultimate example of splendid but vacillating obstinacy, is impartial and unsympathetic, even to coldness. But whether or no it be correct, considered from the historical standpoint, it is aye set forth with distinction and the sure touch of conviction.

Heidenstam is always the inspired craftsman in his work. Yet impressionism in any form of art tends to obscurity of outline and purport : and it is as much owing to this as to the intensity of vehement imagination, conceiving mental visuality, and likewise obscuring it in part, that his narrative occasionally fails in clearness and cohesion. His defects are the defects of his method.

In these tales, the subject matter has been closely followed, not literatim nor with an eye to the nuances of style, but with as much attention to the truthfulness of its presentment as to its right array in fitting English. I trust that language and form are such as the author himself would have used were he an Englishman.

A. TEGNIER.

CHAPTER I.

THE GREEN GALLERY.

In the castle-quarter, where the firewarden sold brandy and beer, a tall narrow-shouldered customer had been cast out headlong upon the steps; his pewter pot, thrown after him, rolled down before his feet. The worsted stockings of the man were dirty and darned. His neck-cloth was pulled up about his mouth and unshaven chaps. He kept his hands behind him, thrust into the back pocket of his coat.

"Throw out Ekerot. The idiot!" cried the firewarden, "He has blown tobacco into the beer, and struck Peter Malermeistar with a darning needle; he's full of every kind of mischief and devilry! Then close-to the table; order has come to shut the gates. The King is dying."

Old Haakon, a lifelong retainer of Charles XI., was one of those present. He bore a friendly countenance, and in his tight-fitting livery walked so bowlegged, that he looked as if he had just got off horse-back. He lifted the pewter pot, and in an amicable fashion thrust it under Ekerot's arm.

B

" I will see the officer home," said he, " or the lieutenant, or whatever he calls himself ! "

" Lars Ekerot is Captain in the King's Navy ! " answered Ekerot, " and far travelled and cunning in tongues, too, is he ! But for all this, the folk here know not enough to make any allowance for him. I'll complain about them, I'll make a charge ; that I shall ! Have I not told you : Heaven will soon rain judgment on this place, and every rafter in it will be ablaze ? Corrupt councillors and unjust judges— false testimony and many miseries—these have become our daily bread. The Lord's Anger lies heavy on the Land."

" My good sir, lieutenant or captain, in all truth you need prophesy no worse misfortunes than those which God has already laid on us ! Fires are breaking out everywhere in the outskirts of the town ; for ten autumns, now, we've had barren harvests and famines ; and this year a ton of rye already costs ten silver rix-dollars. The fodder, too, 'll soon be at an end in the Royal Stables ; and the grain ships lie outside, fast in the ice ! "

Ekerot went with him along the staircase, and looking about. His beady, restless eyes did not notice anything. Now and then he stood still, cackling and talking in an undertone to himself.

Through the windows they saw the Burg beneath them, with the raised *perron* and its statues, and the sentinels tramping up and down the Trumpeters' Gallery. Behind its snowy towers and roofs small black groups of men were to be seen travelling on the ice between Kungsholmlandet and Söder ; and the setting March sun, shining athwart the windows of a chamber in the left wing, made as it were the concentrated lustre of the Crown glistening there.

" Yes ! " murmured Ekerot, " yes ! it must all, all, burn ! all that has been our shame and our greatness. Charles's Wain I have seen shine bright in the night sky, and when to-night I sit, pipe in hand, amid the tobacco smoke, I note wonderful stars foretelling that the old ordering of the world is out of place. In Hungary and Germany swarms of Arabian locusts have fallen. The fire-spouting mountains throw up burning stones. In February, two years gone, we had green grass finger high in Djurgaarden, and heard the birds of spring merrily singing : but we were using sledges again in May. Hoar frosts whitened the corn in August: yet in September I plucked strawberries on Essingen. In such times it is, that the Lord God opens the eyes of His own, so that they may perceive hidden things."

" God-a-mercy, say not so ! " stammered Haakon. " Does he give this sight, then, to folks asleep or waking ? "

" When one is between the two ! "

" Every word I promise to tell to the King, if you, lieutenant, would give me the full truth of what you have seen and know. Look there, at the two windows with their shutters drawn-to ; I was inside that room not more than two hours ago ! The King sits there, in a chair padded round with pillows and thick coverings : he is so shrivelled and little now, that his face is all nose and lips; he cannot raise his head at all. Poor, wretched King! what agonies he must suffer, and he, too, only in his forties! When he was wont to come limping through the chamber, I was glad if I could get away; but, for all I'm one of the least of his servants, he would immediately take me around the neck, and, streaming with tears, affectionately press me to him; I do not believe he feels warmer towards his son or his wife! When he does send for him, he is usually chary of speaking, and sits and looks at him. He only talks about the Country now, always about the Country. A week ago, I saw some documents of his concerning the tax on house-surveys and town-dues and like affairs; and now he has written his last and secret advice for the son's use, and put the letter safe away into a locked iron box; and as soon as anyone comes into the room his eyes seem to mean the very same as his words always do. 'Help me, help me, to keep the Country, to make my son worthy and wise. The Country! The Country.'"

Haakon passed his hand over his forehead; and they continued along the passage from window to window.

"In that room yonder, to the left behind us, her Majesty lives, the Queen-widow. For the last few days she has shut herself up, and not even Tessin, the Master Builder, will get in to her. No one knows how she busies herself; but I am thinking she spends the time at cards! There is a tinkling and clinking of trinkets against the card table, and a swishing and rustling of lace and silks . . . and the Spanish cane with the gold knobs on it falls on the floor. . ."

" . . . And the lady in-waiting, beautiful Hedwig Stenbock, does she not take a hand in it ? "

" She may well leave it alone, for she's been long married, and is old and wicked, and at home within four walls ! My good sir, you only live in that which was, and which ought to be ! "

" Possibly ! " and Ekerot gazed craftily and with insinuation at the new north wing, newly reconstructed by Tessin, the previous one having been razed to the ground. Some of the scaffolding yet stood there, the rough spruce twigs still on the ends of the topmost baulks.

" Well, who lives on the other side, now ? No one, not even the devil, eh ! and henceforth, too, none 'll live there,—I know as much ! Why could not everything remain as of old ? Understand, that according as every man has a soul, so in every old house there lodges some evil spirit or other, something of the Devil, that aye will break out and come to no good, when one begins to use mattock and trowel ! Do you bring to mind the Green Gallery that formerly ran down there, under the roof over the old Castle Church ? It was there my eyes were first opened ! Yes, yes, I'll tell you. I will tell you everything, if you'll come home with me, and later on keep your promise to recount every word to the King."

They had now passed out at the Castle gates, and were crossing the bridge above the burying ground. Just then a courier, with a leather satchel at his back, was dismounting. Through the tramping of feet and words of command was to be heard his answer to the many questions: "Six mile round, north of Stockholm, only three men seen. . . . Sitting by the road-side, devouring a dead beast . . . in Norrland a pound of meal mixed with crushed bark costs four silver rix thalers. The soldiers are starving; the regiments are reduced to half-strength!"

Ekerot nodded in assent, as if he was long acquainted with the entire state of affairs. Then together with Haakon he held on again, the pewter pot under his arm, his hands in his back pocket.

As they were climbing the stairs to his chamber in Traangsund he threw a suspicious sidelong glance at Haakon, and on inserting the key closely examined whether or no the door had been opened in his absence. The room was spacious and empty. At the window stood a cage with a squirrel therein. On one of the walls a number of various coins were fastened in rows: bright thalers, and great and small copper coins, a five ducat piece, and also a couple of notes, worthless for thirty years past.

"The fool," said Ekerot, "hides his treasure so cunningly, that he cannot watch it; but I will always keep mine before my eyes, so I can quickly tell it into a bag when the great fire comes!"

From a corner he drew forth five sulphur-tipped wooden matches, laid them on the hearth, and kindled them by means of flint and steel. Then he and Haakon ceased blowing up the fire; and as no chairs were there, seated themselves on the floor in front of the blaze.

"And now let us hear the tale," said Haakon.

Said Ekerot, "Never have I seen anything so full of horror as that Green Gallery! It was the time when I was an officer in the Navy. Nowadays they throw into my pocket the paltry pension of two hundred and fifty thalers, and let me be: I can take it all! They hunted me out of the Service for fear I had become the Admiral; and Hans Wachtmeister wished to become that! 'The fellow's mad,' he yelled on deck, when I asked him, most courteously, first to bow before ordering me into the rigging; so then, all was ended as far as I was concerned. 'Mad Ekerot,' I was always called, wherever I went. Yes, it is ever the same in the world. A poor comrade carries a friend to the grave, then his master; and in the end, this and that one, for a bare doit; he gets himself an oilskin cap and a long black cloak; and when he is in a hurry his lists of dead slip out of his pocket; and the children take to their heels, weeping and yelling, 'The undertaker! The undertaker!' But, though one can become such terrifying wraith, we are all kneaded out of the same common clay.

"And now this, that I will say, you must repeat word for word to the King himself.

"At the time which I talk about, I was sent into drawing and design. One day before that quarrel with Wachtmeister, I was ordered, according to gracious command, to take a second with me, named Nils, and instal myself in an empty lumber-room above the Papists' Church in the Castle tower, next the river. Here we were to draw from a defective ship's lantern on Mätar one desired by the queen-widow for her sloop.

"One day as we sat there, playing hazard, and arguing about the lantern, which was designed cursedly wrong, some fun came into my head. Cried I, 'Nils, have you ever seen a dog with five legs?' When Nils but gave a shrug, I continued, 'I have, —in the Iron Mart; it went on four legs, and the fifth it had in its mouth,—but it was not its own!' Nils began to growl, so to tease him I cried still louder, 'Witty you are not! Now we'd like to see very much if you're mettlesome? I wager this pot, full of the right good Spanish wine, and a ducat at the bottom of it all, that I will go all alone through the Green Gallery at curfew!

"He answered, 'I know, that when you take a brisk notion into your head, you're not to be put off it; yet I would not have it laid to my avarice that I could not agree to the wager; so, Ekerot, I take it up as you wish! But I would like to justify myself ever so little to your old mother, if any harm come to you, so I'll go home now. In the day-time, this place is heartsome enough to look at, but at night-time it becomes lonely here; I'd rather sleep in the most wretched hole outside.'

"I called him a coward, and let him go. When by myself I noticed the darkening was already setting in; and to harden myself I went quickly down the stairs to the Green Gallery, and peered through the key-hole. The green tint was painted on most of the place, so that the older and ruddier colour lightened underneath it. Along the walls stood all sorts of furniture out-of-date, and so stored here; I saw presses, and chairs, and paintings of dogs and horses, and farther on a bed with curtains drawn together. Along the sides were recesses and dark corners, where the rain dropped down from the leaking roof.

" It was about the time of Walpurgis, thus the night somewhat clear, and this gave me a certain feeling of security, so that I durst set myself down on the stairs to wait. I knew that strange creatures had their lurking places there, beneath the flooring of the Gallery. The servants called them Witches of the Night, because it needs always be pitch dark afore they heaved up the loose boards and showed their heads. They were no larger than thirteen-year-old children, and wholly brown and naked, and possessing the shape of woman. Often and often would they climb on the presses, and swing themselves round by means of their arms; and anyone who had the misfortune to encounter one of them, most surely must die before the year ran out. Well, as soon as I hear the bells, I opened the door. I took one step; but my fear was so big, that I stood still, with both hands on the door-posts, and staring into the deepening twilight. Through a hole in the boarded windows I could see out, as far as the Tower on Brunkeberg, and this so heartened me, that I straightway stepped into the Green Gallery, so that the ringing might not stop before I was come back. As long as the bells rang out, the creatures of darkness had no power.

"When I was halfway, maybe, I suddenly saw something dark glide in front of me, out from behind the bed-curtains, and slip down into an old elbow-chair, as if to hide itself or awaiting me: I felt as if my knees failed me, and I heard the echo of my scream shrilly repeat itself. Hear you now! From that very moment my eyes became opened, and since then men call me ' Idiot.'

"Against the light from the window I saw it was a man. He did not remain stiff-still like to myself. He instantly seized me by the arm, and hissed between his teeth ' Figlio di un cane! Spy? Servant of the Queen-Widow?'

"'God be praised!' I stammered, when I knew it was a man, and understood by his shaking, unapt, fumbling hold of me that he was as much affrighted. Likewise I perceived he went bare in his stocking-soles, and had thrust the shoes into the breast of his coat.

"I collected myself, and told him of my innocent notion. In the end he believed me.

"'Such an accursed, rotten old hole,' growled the man, to conceal his perturbation. 'There is so much rain dripping down from the roof that my feet are wet. As I do live, a new house should be built here. . . . My good man, can you find the way? Then help me through this maze to the Ballet Hall. Who I am is a matter of indifference to you!'

"'Certainly!' I replied. 'Although I do know Tessin the master-builder, and Chamberlain, perfectly well!'

" He bowed, and took me by the coat-tails, so then I turned myself and went before him; at bottom, I believe, each was equally glad to have met the other. When we had found the way down to the Hall, he ordered me to stay outside; but I heard the Witches jumping in the darkness behind us, and put my hand on the door-lock, so that I could open the door, and unperceived slip in behind him. Through the window one looked down on the river. Within the Hall a number of side-scenes were leant against the walls, painted finely with trim woods and white-walled temples.

"Tessin remained standing in the middle of the Hall, and softly clapped his hands.

"A woman rose up from behind the staging, and opened a small dark lanthorn: she was Hedwig Stenbock, the Queen-Widow's great maid-of-honour. So now, you may understand how the foreign fop has climbed so high!

" Hedwig, my dearest on earth!' said he. ' We're just searching for your room. No answer, ma chere?'

" Hedwig Stenbock was at that time nigh almost on five and thirty, and she approached him so stiff and full of ceremony, that I thought she had neither heart nor soul; but suddenly she changed; the red blood flushed her cheeks when he embraced her. Then I forgot myself and cried fairly loud. 'Aha! aha!' Tessin lurched about; but he was so drunk with desire, that he only drew together his eyebrows in rebuke.

"He explained my presence.

" ' We must have an accomplice at any rate; and Ekerot can be as capable as anyone, at that! If he understands to keep his mouth shut, he'll not go unrewarded!'

"Thereupon he bade me take the lanthorn and go through the empty council chambers—thanks for the honour; and again, by a way which he directed me, down to where the Court Ladies of the Queen-Widow lived. May you aye sleep in peace, my fair ones! And as soon as I had made sure that nothing was a-go there, I was to come back and advise them.

"But I had to tell something wholly different when I returned in safety. I had had to hear the Witches rioting behind the door of the cabinet; and see them leap with small sparks of fire playing from their hands before the Chamber of Archives, where the State papers are kept in chests along the wainscotting. But at last I had found the night attendant of the Queen-Dowager. He was sitting in the corridor by his hand-lamp, and fast asleep, his shoulders against the wall.

" ' He has been sent for, after I left!' Said Hedwig Stenbock, standing proud and stiff as ever. 'He has no idea, the bird has flown though. But, how now to get back?'

"She thrust Tessin's arm away from her, and became very thoughtful.

" ' I have long feared this, and thought over it. Scandal will break out about us, to-night. Her Majesty herself is jealous!'

"Tessin clutched the air as if at seeming swords and daggers, and his eyes sparkled.

"'Jealous? About me? She is forty years old, and grey-haired already; her voice is as coarse as a man's! Should I, then, always be hearing of this madness? Before whom should I have laid my works, from whom should I have sought protection, if not with Sweden's Hedwig Eleonora.' He bows. 'But fear not, my dearest, no shame shall cloud your name; to-night you accompany me; we can speedily get a sledge; . . . and a little later. . . . Addio! I have friends in Italy!'

"'God in Heaven is my witness,' she answered, 'that I am aye ready to follow you, wherever you go; and from folk I ask nothing, but rather would be with you. Yet first must we take care and examine what is discreet, with a trusty friend and protector. I think on Erik Lindskiöld, he sits and drinks with the King to-night. Ekerot can go down by the Burg court-yard to the little staircase leading from the King's Chambers, and wait there till Lindskiöld appears. Then he will ask him, with many excuses, to come here at once . . . to me.'

"Tessin motioned me away with his hand: I did not heed him, but found a delectable pleasure in obeying so noble a lady.

"The night was already far-spent when I came back with Lindskiöld. He had questioned me closely about the whole affair. He shook his periwig; cursed in a friendly fashion; laughed loud, and behaved as if the whole castle belonged to him.

" When he was come into the Hall, he bent on one knee, and threw his hat into the air, and cried! 'Dear folks, are you wholly decided then? You would inflame love, then run away and laugh at them all that guard you? Your passion begets suffering then, and no joys? Pish! Pish! A master architect, an adventurer—not without censure either, of some recent nobility—hopes to win our beautiful Lady-in-waiting. All woes and sorrows began that morn when mother Eve stood in Paradise, nude, new-made, and beautiful, and Adam awoke, and full of hot admiration cried, Madam I congratulate you, for the birth-day!'

" 'Damnation, he is almost tipsy!' muttered Tessin to her. 'C'est ce que l'on appelle l'esprit suédois! Lindskiöld is drunk.'

" 'Only a very little! He is in the right mood.'

" Lindskiöld heard them not, but continued speaking; his voice echoing through the great place. 'For a long time past I have had some suspicion about this; and the noble descendant of the Stenbocks will take it in good part! But to travel to Italy? bah! The country for the Chamberlain lies here: it needs his genius! Look me in the face, sir, and tell me if you can run away from the drawings, spread out by you on my table, or if there's anything in the world so dear to you as your art?'

" 'I am resolved to marry the Chamberlain, and there the matter is!' quoth Hedwig Stenbock.

" Lindskiöld laid his hand above his heart.

" 'Certainement! certainement!' cries the Dowager! 'I myself will make a wreath of blossom off my

own lime trees! I have no forefathers buried in the
vault beneath the church-vane: Schmied was my
father's name, and what was he? Plainly a burgo-
master of Skenning! Now if only it was the Chamberlain who came out of Skenning, how would he
have been forced to make shift to build? A new
castle for the King?—after the Skenning sort! That
town? Puh, I had enough hatred for it! However,
because he is what he is, the Chamberlain is both
supercilious and without any cunning!'

"Lindskiöld took Tessin by the arm, then he drew
himself up, erect and haughty, with a bearing as if he
had suddenly thrown aside a distasteful masquerading
costume.

"'His passion will cool down in a month or so!
Now, as a beginning, the Chamberlain kisses the hand
of her he delighteth to honour, and goes back three
steps, makes an obesiance, then follows me. Be
calm! my word goes far, you know, in the King's
ear! Then Ekerot returns to the attendant of the
Queen-widow, blows out his lanthorn, gives him a
right sound thumping on the ear, and throws his
shoes behind him; so then the man believes it is all
owing to the witches, and our worthy lady can reach
her room in tranquillity. However, it is further
determined that in a short time she betake herself
on a journey to Pomerania: the Chamberlain meets
and marries her there, without any unnecessary stir.
Her Majesty I'll take upon my own conscience—the
accursed misfortune—I mean the Queen-widow, that
cunning woman . . . aye, the devil himself can-

not manage her.   But I have heard how they laid the
unjust hand on the unfriendly nobles at the recovery
of the crown lands; and know how much she gained
from that; and will put her in mind thereon.   New
times are coming, you may be certain!   Ah, my
dear children, my dear children, if you only knew how
the heart grows big with anxiety when one is at the
rudder of state, and steering towards far-off beacons,
the very names of which one durst not even mention
before the King.   But believe my words, and do what
I say.   Here, then, where we now stand the Chamberlain will some day establish his immortality!'

"Tessin, all bewildered, took Lindskiöld's hand
and carried it to his lips.   When I had done my errand
on the attendant, he offered me, with a grimace, these
two notes, there on the wall. 'Now,' said he, 'he
has the promised reward of his silence.'

"But after this adventure all my visions and my
ill-luck began, and, whenever, being unwell, I had to
stay at home, my vapours were the common talk of
every quarter; and I had gout, too, consumption,
asthma, even St. Vitus's dance, and a buzzing in my
head.   Even at the time I took the notes I was aware
they had been out of circulation many years!   And
now give a strict account in the presence of His
Majesty the King of all I have told you."

Ekerot wished to say more, but there came a
sudden knocking on the door, and a messenger called
Haakon to the King, whose condition had changed for
the worst.

A little time after, it was the day following Easter,

the people were informed that the King was in the last extremity, but Ekerot only nodded in his accustomary fashion, as if it all were already known to him. A multitude of starving men and women, to whom work had been promised outside on the neighbouring land, stood in the snow on the streets, shelterless and desperate. With his hands in the back pocket of his coat, Ekerot went from group to group, listening intently to their murmurs, and nodding and nodding again in corroboration. He wrote down predictions concerning the coming night, which he delivered to the Court Chaplain, Wallin, calamities he prophesied were wont to evince themselves during the hours of darkness, so that they might make plain to the envisioned Blessèd that which is disguised and hidden by the light.

It was on a windy April day, shortly after he had shoved his last prediction under Wallin's outer door, that Ekerot seated himself at his window, and talked to his squirrel. Then he bit at a dry pear which he took out of a chest of drawers. Now, as he sat there, he heard, all of a sudden, alarms and clangings of bells, and when he stretched himself out of the window he saw the Castle roof enveloped in fiery smoke. He turned about and began to take his money off the wall, carefully he counted it into his pocket. He trembled, and his teeth chattered; but with the squirrel under one arm, and the pewter pot below the other he stumbled down the stairs to the street. He got thrust against the walls of the houses by the crush of folk, and out of wind, so he stood still and stared up at the

c

Castle, where the licking flames were already beating among its brittle rafters. Soon the three great wings were blazing like enormous heaps of wood; the thunderous roaring of the flames overpowered the pealing of bells and the rolling of the drums.

"Behold, behold," cried he, "the witches now must flee into the bright day. See how they fly in files along the ridges of the roof, with fire in their hands. They climb the roof of the Tower, and hop down on Tessin's new gable; 'twas he disturbed their ease! They will be consumed. This is but the beginning. All shall be burnt to the ground. All. All."

Soldiers and servants forced their way out over the Castle bridge, between casks of water and furniture and pictures. Under the two lions, upon which rested the Royal Escutcheon above the fold of the great door, appeared Hedwig Eleonora, the mother and grandmother of the two Karls. Two courtiers supported her; they almost had to carry her, for she sank down to the ground, and constantly desired to remain still and look back. The mantilla over her silver-grey hair was motioned by the wind, and the following instant it swathed her face like to a dark veil covering the weeping eyes, the proud aristocratic nose, and vividly rouged cheeks.

"The bier burns beneath the body of thy son," Ekerot cried, and stretched forth his hand, "and the Throne burns, upon which thy son's son is mounted, and before thou closeth thine eyes will the whole kingdom be buried below ashes. Thou needst remember no more than this : but that he was born with blood upon his hands." Then he violently forced his way through the press, alongside the walls of the houses, towards Traansund.

The sparks of the conflagration arose heavenward like stars. Behind the walls of the Church-court one saw the great Tower of the Castle, the Three Crowns rearing itself four stories higher than the highest roof, in each of its stories now carried by fire, dense smoke was puffing out through the empty window openings like to puffs of cannon smoke. There are the witches, thought he, making glad over the victory, while the Burg of the Vasa Kings is being consumed.

Again and again the smoke wrapped round the ancient emblems of the Kingdom ; again and again, up there in the dizzy height, those three Golden Crowns glimmered out like three storm-birds rocking themselves on the wing. The bellringers in the Church of St. Nicholas climbed up the stairs to save their great bell, but when they heard the roaring of the fires, as the floors and galleries gave way, and the great Tower with the Escutcheon broke into a downfall of stones and mortar, they turned and escaped.

Seized with fright, women and children began to sob, and then to run. It was they who said that at Söderport they saw a man with a squirrel in his hand and a pewter pot under his arm, making stealthily into the farther country, and he was softly singing to himself an old penitential Psalm.

CHAPTER II.

THE CONVERSION OF THE KING.

In the Great Church of Stockholm the audience had arisen in their pews, and were gazing towards its entrance. Before it Karl XII. of Sweden was alighting from the state carriage.

He was a handsome youth, something thin and undergrown. His plumed hat appeared comically small, its brim being up-turned ludicrously high over his large and disordered peruke. When he thrust it under his arm, his mien was nervous and constrained. He walked with a mincing step and knees bent somewhat according to the prevailing mode. His eyes he kept groundwards. He was finely attired in a mourning suit, its facing of ermine, his gloves were tipped with the same, and on his high-heeled shoes of Cordova leather he wore buckles with rosettes.

Ill at ease by reason of the many inquisitive glances, he took his seat beneath the Golden Crown. He sat stiffly there, fronting the communion table, unable to fix his mind on the holy ceremony. When, at last, the Pastor mounted the pulpit, and with a stout blow on the reading desk, gave out a roll of murmured words, the King flushed deeply as if caught in the very act of remissness. Yet, soon his thoughts again escaped him, following their own trend ; and he began to pluck at the black tails of the ermine to gloss over his embarrassment.

" Look there ! " said a woman, sitting in a pew at the farther end of the Church. " He should have felt a little more of the fatherly rod, he should !   Perhaps, though, the devil has bitten his finger ! "

" Hold your tongue, you jiber, he has smuggled himself into a better seat than you have come to ! " her neighbour replied, shoving her out head first into the passage.

At the door stood the Beadle with his staff ; his duty was to go the round of the congregation and arouse any sleepers. As he now raised his hands in protection of himself, he let his staff fall to the floor ; the clatter echoed up the Church as far as the nobility. Some turned round to view the brawl. The Pastor hastened to deliver the following exordium :

" Peace, I say, the Christian peace, and whither does it tend, with its delectable, Heavenly manna ? Perchance into the households of the folk. Thereupon it keeps firm and steadfast. And perchance it is found in God's own house, or with your Majesty, in your very person ! Whosoever find, feed ye well upon it.   And thus, I say unto you, thou Prince of this earth : Strive ever towards peace and love. Encourage not unto discord that sword set into your hand by God Almighty for the protection of your subjects."

At this the King's face became blood red, and in

a confused manner he laughed outright. Hedwig
Eleonora, the Queen Dowager, opposite him, herself
nodded and cackled, but the young Princesses laughed
most. Of course Ulrica Eleonora sat stiff as ever ;
yet Hedwig Sophia stretched out her lanky neck, and
held her prayer-book before her mouth, glad in the
consciousness that now the keen-eyed dames were
eyeing her fine gloves.

The King grew bolder by degrees, and looked
around him. In what a strange temple of God he
found himself! The entire Church was stored with
furnishings and works of art saved from the fire ; only
the middle aisle was unencumbered. In the corner,
facing the communion table, stood the paintings of the
Last Judgment and the Crucifixion, the canvasses
rolled up together, and there behind the sarcophagus
he recognised the plumes and green tapestry hangings
of that bed in which his father had breathed his last,
propped up with pillows.

Yet this recollection did not touch the King. He
had felt for his parent scarce any other feeling except
that of fear. He had looked on him more as the
representative established by God than as a dear and
near kinsman. In his thoughts, likewise his speech, his
fondest appellation of him was only " the old King."

Like two bees in quest, his eyes roamed over the
numerous well-known objects, and in the end they
rested a long while on the last pillar in the Church.
There, buried some years ago under the flagstones, lay
his tutor, Nordenhjelm, the good-hearted old Norco-
pensis, on whom he had been wont to cling with

childish affection.   He recalled the early lessons in
the wintry mornings, when he sat beside him cipher-
ing the four rules, and occasionally snuffing the wicks,
or when Nordenhjelm told him about the heroes of
Greece and Rome.

Since the death of the Old King he had been going
about like one in a dream.   He knew it to be un-
seemly of him to show any lightsomeness, and that
he was to expect nothing but demonstrations of grief
from others ; yet at the same time he was well aware
that in secret folk considered the affair very collectedly
indeed, and sought to win his favour while he was
trying to amuse himself as quietly as possible, now
through this, now through that.   Even His Excellency, Piper himself, could suddenly dry his tears
and implore him not wholly to renounce youthful
recreations, but on the contrary to take part in a
hawking party.

The stern, lugubrious countenances now on all
sides so wrought on him, that tears came unwittingly
into his eyes.   Yet out of the hidden depths of the
boy's soul mounted the dizzying, intoxicating incense
of victory; for these grim, stubborn old nobles, whom,
formerly, he had feared and evaded, he had found
unexpectedly submissive and obedient.   Sometimes,
as they sat at the board, their faces mournful as ever,
he had thrown fruit pips at their lachrymose features,
and observed how thereupon everyone did laugh, yet
directly afterwards they would approach the Queen
Dowager and surround her with their most sorrowful
selves.

The fire, with its scenes and danger, had been to him of extreme interest and suspense. Yes, altogether that had been the most enjoyable day of his life hitherto! The terrors of the others, the swooning of his grandmother, had only combined to make the rare spectacle more singular and unprecedented. Everything was ended now, so far as former times were concerned : the Old King was gone, the Burg a place of ashes ; it would be the new, it would be all that after which Sweden was hankering, which should now arise with him, even as a flame of fire. And so thinking, he sat there solitary, and only fourteen years of age.

Now it seemed to him that Nordenhjelm was standing there, in the pulpit, behind the Pastor, prompting his discourse. The Pastor had shaken but for a little time the cap and bells, as it were, to place himself on a more intimate footing with his audience. Then he had addressed himself to his sovereign, and, before the great congregation, charged him with his high calling, most earnestly and strenuously. He adjured him in the name of God not to permit himself the toleration of parasites and flatterers lest self-love and arrogance become his portion, but willingly to devote his every action to the faithful people of Sweden, so that he too in later years could close his weary eyes in peace, and, attended by the benedictions of all, enter into the Eternal Glories of God.

The voice of truth rang clamant throughout the vaulted arches of the church ; and the young King was moved almost to tears. Anew he engaged his thoughts on other and indifferent things; but each word of the Pastor smote his open, childish heart; and there he sat with bowed head.

It was a relief to him when he was again brought to Karlberg. There he shut himself into his chamber. Not even an imperative command from the Queen-Widow could induce him to appear.

In his anteroom lay the books used by him in hours of study, now become increasingly rare. Already he liked to philosophise over the problems of existence. Thirst for knowledge was overpowering him; yet likewise had he begun to contemn learning and lore of books, and to yearn after life itself, even like to the lusty and daring troubadour.

The topmost book treated of geography. He turned over its leaves here and there, and threw it aside. Then, irascible and at random, he took up the next volume. In the end it seized his attention.

This book was used, and tattered at its corners; it contained only a few pages, wherein was that evening prayer which he had been taught to repeat as a child: some of the words and their meanings were wholly gone from his memory. But, when he now saw the well-known letters again, he only required to read them over three or four times to know them once more by heart.

That night he partook of one tassie of beer; and then the servants of the bedchamber began to undress him. He wanted so strongly to hide his agitation, that they imagined he was but very tired. After they had removed the periwig off his short wavy hair, and he clad in his shirt stepped into the great bed, he looked just like a little girl.

His dog, Pompey, crouched down at his feet. At the end of the bed the servants placed a lit candle within a silver basin full of water; for the King feared the dark. It was also their custom to leave the door of the outer chamber ajar, and that a page or play-mate spent the night there. This night Karl ordered in a firm voice that his door was to be shut, now and hereafter. When the servants heard this they began to wonder and be alarmed, noticing, too, that he was agitated.

" Ah, bah! " growled old Haakon, trusty servant of his father's time. He stubbornly continued to treat the King as a child. " What's that for ? "

" It is as I have spoken," was answered in a decided tone. " And from to-morrow I will no longer need the night-light."

The servants bowed, and stepping backwards left the room. But when Haakon had shut the door, he set himself without, on the threshold. He heard the King tossing hither and thither on his bed. On moving himself up on his knees he saw obscurely through the door-lock, by the light of the candle, that his young Sovereign was now sitting up in bed.

The night wind swirled in gusty eddies along the terraces and among the creaking linden trees; but all was still and peaceful within the Castle. Then it was to the astounded Haakon that he heard a low murmuring voice. With difficulty he distinguished some of the words; he became attentive, and gave close ear. It was the King offering up that prayer of early childhood years.

" Teach me, O Lord, to rule myself, so that I become not corrupted by the tongue of flattery unto waywardness and pride of self, and thus fall short in that esteem which I am owing to Thou, O God, and to man."

Old Haakon bowed the knee and folded his hands in prayer. And in the silence of the sleeping Castle and through the low siftering of the wind came again the words of the King.

" Though I be a king's son and heir to a mighty kingdom, yet constantly will I keep in mind that these are but the signal favour and blessing of God, and for that reason must I apply myself towards wisdom and virtue, so that I may become worthy and fitted for so high a calling. Almighty God, Thou, Thou who puttest Kings of the earth upon their thrones and settest them down likewise, teach me always to walk in Thy commandments, lest I misuse that power bestowed on me, to my own destruction and the oppression of others. According to Thy Holy Name, O Lord. Amen."

CHAPTER III.

AFTER THE CORONATION.

How weary it was. How tedious the days passed at the little palace. The black-clad Councillors yawned, lolling in their seats, and stared before them as if they were incessantly pondering how it came that they wore like shoes on both feet, and not a top-boot on one and a silken shoe on the other. They gaped, and without, in the passages, on the stairs, the servants gaped, too. And crowded into the great kitchen the cooks tasted the dishes with their fingers, and asked one another if the times were not sour enough to turn even the acrid faces of the Lords in authority.

Before the black state carriage, with its horses and their mourning plumes and rosettes, stood the King's grooms. In Graamunkholm Church, where the old King was buried, the black canopy and hangings were yet in place. The King's chimes echoed far over the land. When at last the coronation procession had wound through the snow-covered streets, every one was in mourning; only the young King wore his purple. And no sooner had the last boom of the guns reverberated over Tyskbagareberg, than the intolerable monotony instantly settled down. . . .

But one gray forenoon, the cook of the Queen Dowager began to caper about. In his hand he held a jar containing some cooked tomatoes. "Ah, good times, good times!" he exclaimed. "We will do something to-day. His Serene Highness, the Duke of Holstein,—it seems he is expected to arrive soon, —has sent a right good present of fruit. His Majesty and the Lady Greta Wrangel have already partaken of some. The Chamberlain, himself, is coming down into the kitchen to give us a hand. Stand ye gaping there, youngsters! Quick. Get a cloth, and polish up that kettle there!"

This little court, at the verge of civilised earth, had now obtained something whereon to sharpen its wits. At table, then, all conversation turned on the tomatoes; every one had something to say concerning their smell and savour. Afterwards, every one drank heartily; and elderly Councillors forgot rank and distinction, and recounted droll amiabilities to each other.

When the repast was over, the King buttonholed Lars Wallenstedt, the Councillor. He drew him into a window corner, like to leading a panting, growling bear by its nose-ring.

"Tell me," said the King, earnestly, "in what manner should a King sacrifice himself for his people? I cannot forget the sermon, that day in spring!"

Wallenstedt was wont, in speaking, to blow out his lips as if he intended to say, "Puh! puh!"

Accustomed to the King's precocious questions, he answered:

"A Prince must renounce all trifling aims, unite

entire authority in himself, and become the sole token, insignia, the very will of his people. Certainly we did listen unto a very edifying sermon; but did not the Pastor likewise say that subjects should be as the very slaves of their ruler? The Council and the nobles are now striving for the control, since the death of your Majesty's most blessed father. And Oxenstjerna, and Gallenstjerna, and . . . No! but one hears things! And that is the reason why I have consistently sustained your Majesty's desire, even at your tender years, to take the sore burden of the Government off the shoulders of Her Majesty."

When Cronhjelm, now tutor to the King, standing in the recess of the window, heard the words about the sore burden of the Government, he wrote with his finger-tip on the moisture-laden pane: "The yoke of the old woman is like to the fontange, pleasant and light!"

"Yes, yes, my good Wallenstedt!" the King replied, "in my own inmost thoughts I have always felt my will thrust me that way: it must be a man who sits on the throne. Yet, a strange tormenting thing is the will! What is it? To-day I may feel inclined to ride to Kungsör to hunt the bear; but, wherefore? As well could I purpose something clean contrary. Will is like a fixed, fastwelted ring round my heart; out of it I cannot escape! It is master, I am slave."

The wax candles were lit when he entered his own chamber. Upon the table stood the locked casket of iron, into which the old King had confided his last and most fatherly advices. Some few days were yet to elapse before the old and resigning Councillors let the young King slip from their control. Hitherto he had not been able to constrain himself to open the casket. It is true that one night he had violently wrest away its seal, but incontinently had turned away. This evening he felt that his irrevocable decision was now arrived.

As he twisted the creaking key, his old panic of the dark seized him once more; before him, too, he saw, as it had been the metal coffin of his father; and it was as if he were now standing eye-to-eye with the dead. Hurriedly he called Haakon in to him, and ordered him to attend to the fire.

Then he unlocked the box, raised the lid, and with a cold shudder smoothed the cramptly written paper. "Take the authority into your own hand," he read, "and safeguard yourself from the great nobles who surround you, and from those with wives out of France. These all making much ado most fervently seek but their own ends: the best of men oft-times walk solitary in their own gardens." And the King, while reading this disquieting warning, did not observe Haakon leaving the room.

Now he was King in all Swedish lands. Arrogant lords had thronged at his doors to avouch his coming-of-age; they were without ken whether his words savoured of accustomary smoothness or whether spoken of direct and genuine purpose: they loved him, so they averred, dearer than sons and brothers. Yet he could never converse confidentially with these old nobles; they so carefully trimmed every word and gesture, and laid them in the balance of suspicion. And if he might speak in full trust to his elders in knowledge and human nature, they were but a set of nervous, amiable, ancient puppets, ignorant of the main trend of the times. Lonely he was as never heretofore; and, alone, would he sustain the sceptre of his father. In Sweden nought could be above him, and of all Swedish kings he would become the greatest. Had he not received a pledge from the hand of the Almighty, in that He had made him sovereign at so youthful an age, and had given him leave to expect so many years of life. The generation which had incurred His wrath was now passed; it sang in Heaven; it made glad with trump and harp.

The King stood erect; with his hand he dealt a light blow on the edge of the table. Piper was correct; he had declared that Sweden was a big country, with a small ignoble Court, situated at the end of the earth. All was to be changed now! Himself had placed the crown on his head, and so attired had ridden into the church. Did he not receive it from the Lord of Hosts at the very hour of birth, that fine June morning when the bright star, the Lion's Heart, had stood over against the eastern horizon?

Only the hoofs of his horse had trampled holes in the carpets laid on the street, the nobles all had to go on foot; the State Councillors themselves had borne his canopy, and like to the veriest menial served him at meat. Why should he dissimulate, why should he pay honour to them whom he honoured not, even in secret? After all, had he to enlighten them regarding the true tenor of a king's assurance, according to circumstances beyond his control had he taken his oath to the people of Sweden. His real oath as King, he had sworn before God, when standing in silence at the communion table. But, now, now was he ruler over the land of Sweden.

He stepped to the mirror, and in contentment examined the small-pox marks in his fair, girlish skin, and with the fingers squeezed wrinkles of fierceness on his forehead. Then thrusting an arm into the air he straddled himself over a chair, and began galloping round the room. . . " On, on, my men ! Forward for your King. . . Jump! jump! Splendid. Jump! On, on. . ." He was picturing that he was riding over a battlefield towards the enemy, and that hundreds of bullets beat harmless on his breast, and flattening out fell down amid the green grass ; on the neighbouring heights stood spectators, and in the distance the King of France himself was coming on a white horse to greet him, waving his hat.

Beneath, in the salon, the powerful aristocrats of the Kingdom were gathered in earnest deliberation. On hearing the noise they held their peace for a moment, and listened. Cronhjelm, drawing with his finger-tip on the misty window pane, murmured almost loudly, " It is only His Majesty devoting himself to the cares of government. Maybe he is pondering over the gracious recompence he intends to give us for our acceptance of his accession ! " Wallenstedt, puffing out his lips, shot a furious look at him.

When the King had ended his prancing, a thought

D

suddenly came into his head. He stepped to the door.

" Klinckovström ! " he cried. " Klinckovström, can you tell me why I have such a longing to ride to Kungsör to hunt the bear ? "

Klinckovström, a jolly page, with ruddy cheeks and a ready tongue, replied :

" On this account, sire, because it is rough weather, black as pitch without, and no bear has been driven in, and the hunt is not practicable ! Will I give order for horse and linkman ? "

" Have ye anything better to suggest ? "

" Many, maybe, better, but . . . ."

" You are right ! To Kungsör we must ride, even now, seeing that the affair looks impracticable, and because we desire it ! "

An hour later, as the King was riding up Drott-ninggatan, he closely skirted a suburb stretching from the graveyard out as far as a yellow painted hostelry.

An old widow, Mother Malin, kept this house. It was surrounded by a wooden fence, upon which the journeymen from the Castle had drawn triumphal cars, and obelisks, and dancing Italians, while they emptied their beakers. In one corner of it stood a pleasure house, with fireplace and chimney : one of the windows of this little house looked towards Drott-ninggatan, the other into the garden, upon plum trees and flower beds. For some months past Mother Malin had daily carried out food to some habitant, there. But none, no ! even of her old customers knew anything about her guest. And at a public sale of the household gear of an impoverished, but noble, family she had purchased a spinet; of an evening, now, one heard foreign melodies ring out in demure, faint tones from behind the closed shutters.

As now the link-bearers of the King rode nearer, Mother Malin stood at a crack in the paling and looked down the dark street.

" It is himself!" she cried quickly to herself, and turned away to knock hastily on the door of the pleasure house. " The King is coming this way. Quick! put out the light, and look out at the dormer window at him." The next moment the King pricked by in a wild ride.

Said she to herself, " How downy his cheeks are, the dear young King! And how I hear he ought to live a clean and upright life! But why would he do nothing but tempt providence by putting the crown on with his own hands! That was why it was about to tumble off again, and the Oil fell on the Church floor." And she went back slowly to the inn.

That night passed on, and one month succeeded another: in the garden of the hostelry the chestnuts and plum trees behind the currant bushes began to burst into leaf, and the barberries to renew their green. The May-pole was set up again, and the Court went by to Karlberg.

Next to the King sat the Duke of Holstein, who was now here to marry the Princess Hedwig Sophia, sister of the King; and bring the intolerable monotony to an end. As he passed the pleasure house it so came that he, by chance, looked through its wide open window.

The same evening a man with the collar of his cloak turned high for concealment, knocked lightly on the inn door. Mother Malin examined him closely, with some mistrust.

Said she, " He may go to the devil, with his high collar, he may ! "

The fellow laughed loud ; in broken Swedish he replied:

" I stay aboard a German ship down there, and wish only to drink a pot of beer in the garden here ! Quick ! " And with that slipping two pieces of money into her hand he shoved her aside.

She had almost given him a smack in the face, but on hastily counting the money changed her mind. The pot of ale she fetched, and placed it on a table in the garden, then, seating herself behind a half-shut window, maintained an inquisitive eye on her new customer, who sat and supped a little of the ale, traced on the ground with his heel, and looked about him.

After he had remained still some while, and, unob-served he thought, he arose and pulled down the collar of his roquelaure. A goodly young man he was, with a quick, merry face. Slowly he made his way to the pleasure house.

" The rascal," muttered Mother Malin, " I fairly believe he intends to knock."

The door remained barred. He went a few steps further, to the open side window. Here he stopped,

and bowed courteously to someone inside. Then he
swung himself upon the window sill, and began to
converse in low, eager undertones.

Mother Malin lost patience. She came out,
cautiously crept along the gravelled walk, her head
cocked in suspicion ; and raking up all the insolence
she would outpour. Scarcely was she gone a few
steps when the young man strode out upon her from
behind a barberry bush.

Said he in furious anger, "Accursed old hag! get
gone. I am the Duke of Holstein. Not a word
about it!" And so taken aback was she, that she
could answer nothing, but twirled herself round, and
incessantly hit herself on the knee. Even when she
returned to the inn she was still slapping at herself,
scarce able to realise that so great and rare a business
was being enacted under her humble roof.

After this it often occurred that, in the clear
summer nights, when no winds rustled the cherry
trees, the Duke came to the hostelry. The pleasure
house door was never opened for all he tapped so
coaxing ; he durst only set himself outside on the
window ledge. Mother Malin now and then getting
a white ducat slid into her palm, served him there
with ale and wine, and once even with a raisin-and-fig
cake, around which she had inscribed with white of
egg : " Prince, in all the kingdoms, is not thy like."

One night the Duke remained longer than usual,
and from out the pleasure house resounded the notes
of the spinet.

When at last he rose to go, said he, "Power,

power! Yes, they all cry out for that nowadays. Why
should you alone keep silent? Are you doing this
because your father lost his last piece in play at the play.
Adieu, adieu. If you aim in vain at the lion, promise
me that afterwards you open the door to the wolf!"

The Duke stood before the window. A deep sfill-
ness held all around in the inn at the foot of the walk;
every one was abed.

"You do not answer," he continued; "Maybe
from coyness! Give me a sign, a token then, in reply.
A harmony on the spinet means 'Yes'; but if you
play with the tips of the little finger it is 'No,' irre-
vocably, 'No.'"

Tardily he withdrew to the walk. The sky of night
was clear; the land lay without a shadow. He tarried
beside a gooseberry bush, scarching for unripe fruit,
but found none. It was then rang out the soft har-
monious chord. Instantly he drew his hat over his
brows, pulled up the collar of his roquelaure, and with
joyful footsteps hastened away. From this evening
Mother Malin waited in vain for her ducal guest, and
finally in her discontent began counting the ducats
out of her pockets, and cursing herself for not having
extracted more from him by means of some timely
arrangement.

Now, one night, the widow of a barber was buried
in the Klara churchyard, and after the last linkman
was gone, two men remained behind to watch beside
the grave.

"All of us must pay the fine! And there the old
body lies in her coffin, with her nightcap of cambric

and her long ribands, like a duchess, and fine breads and preserves and suchlike stand on the table for folks, but to us they have not sent as much as half a pot of small beer!"

"I see a light. There. Over the wall, in Mother Malin's window! Let us get over and knock!"

They went out and across the street, and clappered on the door. Mother Malin half opened the dormer window.

"Right welcome lads, are ye!" said she, after they had explained. "Nowadays a treat is not to be got all at once! Yet ye can earn a bonny gold piece at this very minute if ye wish?" She opened the window wider, and lowered her voice. "Here, each of ye—a whole carolus. Yes, yes! only mind, you pair, ye both lend a hand to him that gives the coin. Inside here is a page of the royal household; he'll soon come down to you. Now, at break of day, the roisterers up at the Castle usually ride this way. What should the two of ye do, then, but throw the young lord about, and pummel him well, and then take to your heels. That is all."

"Easily done, too!" said the fellows. "The most ticklesome part will be not to lay on too hard, for fear we hurt him!" Then, hearing Mother Malin and the page whispering overhead, they went back to the churchyard gate, and stood there awaiting.

Time passed slowly to them. A star twinkled through the summer night just above the deadhouse. The watchmen on Brunkeberg sounded their calls. At last day began to spring.

A creaking and squeaking came from Malin's stair, and the page descended to them. He walked rather knock-kneed, and was restlessly fingering the clasps of his mantel. A hubbub and a trampling of horses rang out in the direction of Drottninggatan. In front of the cavalcade rode Kluckovström, so drunk that he had to hold on by means of his horse's mane. Behind him one distinguished the King and the Duke of Holstein, and, further behind, ten other horsemen. All had swords in their hands, and, save the King, wore only their shirts. Karl was wild with intoxication, smashed at windows with his blade, tore away sign-boards, and beat on the wooden doors. There were none in the world whom he had to obey! He could now do what pleased him alone, and who durst say one word? At the supper table he had knocked the dishes out of the page's hands, and pelted the others with cream tarts till their clothes looked thick with snow. The intolerable old times were gone. Let the aged lords gape and mutter as much as they liked behind their snuff boxes : they had no more to do now but to play the fool, for his kingdom of old bears he was only consecrating to the joys and freedom of youth. In time all Europe should stand agape, for now 'twas he that was King over the broad leagues of Sweden.

The unknown page, meanwhile, had laid himself on the ground at the door to the churchyard ; the loons were thwacking and smacking and thumping him to their hearts' content, and clutching him by the gullet.

" Who is there ? " cried the King, jumping down among them. The men immediately fled over the graves and round the tombstones. But he was on them, and slashed at one so repeatedly, that the blood began to trickle down his arm. In the end they had to seize planks from the half-filled grave, and defend themselves as best they could; thereupon the King turned away laughing, and ran back to the others.

The unknown was now standing.

"One of us?" queried the King, "why! are you so bedazed that you do not recollect the password of ours, 'Snuff on the periwigs?' Never mind. Sit up there beside our friend Klinckovström, and keep him safe on his Wallachian. Forward!" Then lustily singing and yelling, the shirt-tailed troop scurried on once more, up street and down hill, brandishing swords and making sport of the sleepy-headed cits appearing at their house doors.

When the panes at Marshall Stenbock's commenced to jingle, the celebrated old man himself came in his nightshirt to the window; and, though first bending low, straightened himself to complain that at this rate he would soon require to leave the country.

But the King snatched off his wig, and, throwing it into the air, cut it in two halves with his sword.

"That's life!" the Duke cried. "Hats in the air. Ah, if now we only could get at the languishing beauties, there, moping in their beds! Wigs in the air. Raise up in your stirrups, and let out, away, away over your horses' heads. Like this, you youngsters. The devil will look after you! Vivat Carolus, Rex succorum et scandalorum."

Their shirt tails blew out in the wind. Hats, periwigs, and gloves lay on the street. Their horses, striking sparks from the cobble, dashed forward as if through lightning sheen. When the mad riders reached the Castle they sprang out of their saddles, and let the horses run free. They smashed the hanging lights in the entrance passage, and fired their pistols at a marble Venus.

" Forward," shouted the King. With his following he stormed into the Chapel, where he wrote freely on the pews : " On Sundays the breeches of the folk here should be lined with splinters."

Then the Duke knocked on the floor, and asked for attention. Klinckovström, lying on the communion table, was playing dice ; he took hold of his mouth to keep it still.

"My dear hearers," began the Duke, "nothing would add more to the pleasure of this our solemn festival, than if our noble and much-loved cousin, at this morning hour, now give us a hint concerning the little affairs of his heart. But let us digress upon the ardent fair. Let us consider that fair damsel from Bavaria, who with her sweet mother journeyed hither, although after the burning of the Castle scarce a lodging was to be found. ' Huh-huh !' cries the owl. She is only older than your Majesty by some eight little summers. Or let us speak of the Princess of Wurtemberg, who already has shown her great love. Or consider the Princess of Mecklenburg-Grabow, who, it seems, at present is hastening here with her little mother. Or the Prussian Princess, older by only two tiny sweet-pea years. Or the Danish Princess,

the darling little gold-bird, older than yourself but
five short, rosy years. All, one with another, have
they hastened to the wooing, and that with all the
blandishments and adornments of their countenances
and persons; for love torments them greatly!"

The King grew angry.

"Have I not aye declared," he replied, "that no
man need think of marrying till he is forty!"

When the Duke noticed his confusion, he winked
to the page from the inn, and again rapped on the
floor with his sword.

"Good! the King of Sweden will share his glory
and the love of his people with none but the brave
and joyous. Snuff on the periwigs! Were I King, I
would first terrorise all the parents, and then summon
the fairest of their daughters to our carousals. The
devil! Wouldn't they sit on our saddles before us,
eh, and take part in the fun, till the cock crowed
thrice. God strike me dead on the spot!—I can
speak no more. Put your knees against the pews.
Hack and smash away at them, lads, stamp them to
the floor. Good God, bring water, the King is ill.
Water or wine. Ay, wine! wine!"

The King was now pallid. He thrust his hands on
his brows. It mattered not to him that the features
of the others were inflamed, and themselves unsteady
on their feet. In reality none were so dear to him
that he should grieve. What could it have to do with
him if they did drunkenly revile each other. No
person durst insinuate that about him—him, God's
own anointed!

" Now, that is enough, lads ! " he cried, attempting to sheath his sword.

He observed, however, that he had lost its scabbard. Calmly he stuck the weapon through the stuff of his coat, and went with firm steps to the door.

The unknown page the Duke took by the arm, and, making some signs with his hands, whispered into his ear. The page hurried away behind the King, opened the door for him, and followed him down the stairs.

Thought the King, whether I drink wine again or no, I could not tolerate having it related that I had blabbered out words and hugged my pages ; and in such an affair why should any one think better of me than of the others ? And, after all, wine does not taste much better than small beer ; it is all a matter of custom. But, a brave warrior drinks water. So they passed on, through the corridors and down the staircases, to his sleeping chamber.

Here Wallenstedt, with two other important nobles, was already in waiting. Wallenstedt puffed out his lips, he began with :

" It is our wont, sire, to come here about six o'clock of a morning to submit details of government. . ."

" Yes ! if they are concerned with misdemeanour," replied the King, " otherwise I desire no advices. From hence I will consider and determine matters as I think fit."

He was not fiery like his father. He demeaned himself with as assertive a sense of dignity as a well-

born dame on her seat of honour. Smiling and
bowing about him, he so pressed back the lords that
they had to leave the chamber.

"That is our reward for setting a child on the
Throne!" they murmured maliciously into Wallenstedt's ear.

The page closed the doors behind them, with submissive yet disdainful smile. The King was pleased.
He stood leaning against the tester-bed, next to the
chest in which his father had kept jewels and suchlike, and which had been brought up from the
treasure-vault.

"What is your name?" he asked the page. "Why
do you not answer?"

The page breathed quickly. In a confused manner
he hid himself in his clothes.

"Answer me, boy. You surely know full well your
own name? You turn your shoulders so much toward me, that I cannot see your face!"

Now did the page step into the middle of the room,
snatch away the periwig, and toss it on the bedside
table.

"I am called Rhoda . . . Rhoda d'Elleville."

Before him the King saw a young girl. Her brown
eyebrows were sharply pencilled. Her yellow hair
lay ruffled and in curls; about the sensitive mouth
a little pucker cast its shadow.

She leapt to him, she threw her arms round his
neck, and lightly kissed him on the left cheek.

For the first time in his life of seventeen years, self-
possession deserted him. His eyes burned, his cheeks

became ashy-pale, his hands hung helpless, powerless. He only saw that the unbuttoned coat left her bosom open.

She held him in a fast embrace, and pressed a long kiss on his mouth. He did not return it ; he offered resistance. At first he raised his hands, then thrust her arms, like a ring, up over his head. Stammering and bowing, and with many compliments, he stepped aside. Stiffly he bowed, clacking his heels together every time, bowed and bowed again, always increasing the distance between them.

" Pardon. Pardon."

How often had she not rehearsed every word of her attack. Now she recollected nothing. She spoke wholly at random.

" Mercy, Sire, mercy. It is for God to punish such presumption as mine." She went on bended knee upon the carpet. " Sire, I have seen you on horseback from my window. In my dreams you appeared to me long before I had travelled the long way hither. You, my King, my Alexander. . ."

But instantly he had sprung to her side, offered his arm, and, with a grave courtesy beyond his years, was leading her to a chair. " Not so! Not so! I beg of you, seat yourself. Seat yourself."

For a little while she kept his hand in hers, wrinkled her forehead somewhat, and looked him searchingly and openly in the eyes. She gave a ringing, unburdened laugh.

" Well, you are at least a man, Sire. No trace of the preacher in you. You are the first Swede to understand that virtue casts its eyes inward, and squints not wickedly at aught else. Your favourites drink and dice, and dally with the ladies of the chamber, unless you forbid them; yet you yourself hardly pay any heed to it at all. Speak to us, Sire, about chastity."

The perfume of her, the odour from her hair, her body, made him so sick that he almost retched. Contact with her warm hands caused in him a sensation as repulsive as he were touching a rat or cadaver. He deemed himself insulted and lowered, as well the King elected by God, as the man himself, through a stranger touching his clothes, his countenance and hands. One, even a woman, had seized on him as booty, yea, even as a prisoner bound. Whoever so touched him straightway became his foe; one with whom he would fight, aye, cut down in the street for violation of his person.

" When I was still a child," she went on, " my confessor fell in love with me. He wrung his hands, wrestled with himself, and babbered prayers; but I made him play the fool all the same! Sire, you never strive with yourself, how different you are! You are wholly callous, Sire, that is all. Chastity is so inborn with you, that "—she laughed slyly—" I do not even know if one can term it chastity!"

Employing more strength, he sought to release his hand. How had they all been besieging his ear during the last few weeks—the Duke, the pages, even the servants—every one full of the delights of the beautiful and amorous ladies of the chamber. Was this, then, some play behind his back? Could they not leave him in peace.

" Pardon, Mademoiselle."

" I know, Sire, that you can sit for hours turning over Tessin's engravings, and that in particular you pay attention to the pictures of dainty young women. Maybe it is all owing to that love of the beautiful which you have inherited from your great and worthy Aunt, but should it always be so? I am no lifeless picture, Sire!"

Whilst he still continued to bow, he suddenly wrenched himself away with such force, that he dragged her off the seat.

" No, you are a living page, indeed, Mademoiselle! To the page I give order to go down into the Chapel, and send my companions to the east antechamber."

Immediately she recognised that her trick was lost beyond all hope. The little puckers about her mouth became graver and drooping.

" The page must obey!" she replied.

The King grew calm when he was left to himself, only now and then sharp anger blazed across his face. This unexpected adventure had driven the fumes of drink from his brain; and after all the experiences of the night he did not wish to get abed like a mere youngling.

He threw off his coat. In shirt sleeves and sword in hand he betook him to his boon companions.

The east room was blotched over all with dried blood; its floor was splashed with the same; lumps of hair and congealed gore adhered to the portraits hanging upon the walls, their eyes pricked out. From the neighbouring apartment there was to be heard the lowing of a calf.

The animal was brought in, and set in the middle of the floor. The King bit his netherlip to whiteness, then with one whistling blow of his sword beheaded the calf. With blood on his fingers and under his nails he cast its head through the open window out upon the passers-by.

Without the door of the ante chamber, the Duke whispered feverishly to Rhoda d'Elliville.

" So it seems, then, that my good cousin will do nothing through obstinacy. Hjarne, a strange old man, here, talks about compounding a love potion for him; but that will be no good! Had he not inherited the coldness of his father he might become the arch Borgia of Sweden—he, with all his waywardness. If he cannot grow into a demi-god, he'll grow into a devil! When such a bird on the wing finds no pleasure, it demolishes the walls of its very house. Hush, some one comes. Do not forget, now. To-night, at Mother Malin's. And have some raisins and figs at hand."

Behind them trusty Haakon was coming up the stairs, leading two she-goats. He stood still, and held up his hands. Full of fear he groaned.

" What have they done to him ? Never before have I seen such on-goings in the Swedish Household. Almighty God, be merciful, and send us a great misfortune; Sweden can endure neither the present peace nor such a King! "

E

CHAPTER IV.

A MIDSUMMER VENTURE.

THE little maids were standing in the garden, holding a riddle. Near them, sitting on a mossy stone, was their brother Axel Friedrich, idle and almost asleep; twenty years old he was to-day.

His betrothed, timorous little Ulrica, stood beside the juniper bushes, bending their branches down into the sieve. She was lopping off the twigs; and the little maidens with outstretched hands helped to keep them together. The melting snow was dripping heavily from the birches and alders.

"See," cried Ulrica, "there is grandfather himself coming out, in this fine weather!" pointing over to the house.

The little girls began to sing and romp about, then, lifting up the riddle, they turned towards the house. Beating measure with the swinging sieve they trilled:

> "And the birds of the Spring they sing so rarely,
> Come, ye goatherds, come,
> To-night it is, ye dance so merrily."

At the further end of the garden, where the pines begin to encroach, Elias the serf was fetching home the last load of wood from the forest; the water squelched over his wooden shoes. About the yokes of his red-coloured wain, Silfverhorn and Storbonda twigs were stuck plentifully in protection against the witches. He, too, was humming:

> " And the birds sing so clear and joyous
> ' Come, goats, come,'
> This night flowers bloom
> Among your clean fresh straw."

He stopped. Bending over the fence, said he to Axel Friedrich, " The powder smells bad now, when you fire a piece, and the soot in the chimneys is falling down: the thaw will hold!"

The roofing of the house-entry was of turf. In summer time a goat usually browsed thereon, among the house-leek and catch-fly, but at present the snow was still covering it. The old man was sitting beneath its shelter; clad he was in his grey cloth coat with brass buttons.

Ulrica brought the little maids forward to greet him. They were clad in homespun, dyed blue. When they made their curtesy, rings of violet shimmered out in the wet upon the steps.

The old man stroked Ulrica's cheek with the back of his hand. " You will soon grow up, little one, and be a helpmate to Axel Friedrich."

" Oh, if I was only sure of that, grandfather! But here, there are so many things, and important things, too, that one must look after. I am not used to it at all!"

" Yes, yes. Ah, I am very sorry for Axel Friedrich; he lost his parents so soon. There are no kins-

E—2

folk of his alive, save his two aunts, and the old grandfather here. We looked after him to the best of our abilities : you will soon learn, little one, to take our place. The worst is, his broken health, the good lad ! Ah, dear child, praise God for this sweet spring day and the blessed years of peace." Then the old man handled the juniper twigs, and was glad to find them so damp ; they would take up much dust then.

The two aunts stood at the kitchen window, behind him. They were making ready a mess of beaver-stone oil and bay berry for a sick calf. Both were clothed simply in black, and had white, carefully-smoothed hair."

"Why is Axel Friedrich not with you ? " they asked Ulrica. " Remember, he is to get his favourite dish to-night, at supper—honey groats and syrup ; and afterwards there is to be bacon and onions.

"Yes, yes," cried the old man. " The folk, too, must have this night to themselves."

Ulrica started off to go to the servants' room, where they were cleaning tow. She was not gone many steps, when her timid face, yet small and undeveloped, took on an anxious air. She listened.

"But, Ulrica," the old man was calling, " I do not understand this. Ulrica ! Come here, Ulrica ! "

She again hung up the bunch of keys just taken down from the door-post, and went outside.

"Is that not a horseman, coming this way ? " the old man asked. " I have not been worried with letters, these three months past. I am aye anxious when I get one! See. See! He fumbles about in his pocket."

Then the rider stopped for a second at the foot of the steps, handing him a document, much folded and sealed carefully.

The aunts placed themselves on each side of him in the elbow chairs. They gave him his spectacles; but his hands trembled so much, that he could hardly manage to break the seal. Then all wished to read the letter at once. Ulrica came out of herself so much, that she leant over the old man's arm, and with her little finger pointing out the words, read them aloud.

Of a sudden, she beat her hands together, and stared straight before her, tears welling into her eyes.

"Axel Friedrich, Axel Friedrich," she cried, speeding across the court-yard into the garden. "Axel Friedrich! For God's sake, Axel Friedrich!"

"What do you want?" answered he, throwing aside the liquorice which he was chewing. A full, round face had Axel; a delicate rosy skin, and voice kindly but unspirited.

She remained stock still at first, then seized his hand.

"Do you not know? The order is come that the regiment is to get itself in readiness and join the Colours; for the invasion of the Danes in Holstein!" And with her clinging to him, he came into the house.

"My dear child," faltered the old man. "Ah, that I must now have such a trial! War is come at last."

Axel stood pondering for a few moments. At last he looked up. Said he, " I will not go! "

Restlessly his grandparent tramped up and down, and with him tripped his aunts.

"You are enrolled, my dear lad! The one chance is, that we may be able to buy a substitute."

"That will be done, easily!" Axel replied, in an indifferent tone. And he stepped into the house. But Ulrica trailed herself upstairs, her apron at her eyes, and cast herself upon her bed.

When the honey groats were cooked, and all sat round the board, the old man, as was his wont, desired to weave a hundred meshes on the fish net. But now his hands shook overmuch.

" There must have been some evil ongoings, in Stockholm, there," said he; " the rumours soon spread about.   Ballets, masquerades, and other buffonery seem to have been daily fare with our new King; and when the money was at an end, he began giving away the Crown Jewels. Ay! Our indulgent sovereign must learn another lesson, now!"

Axel thrust away his plate. Lazily he rested his elbows on the table while his aunts and Ulrica cleared away the dishes. His grandfather nodded to himself, and coughed. He continued:

" All these years of peace have only begotten avarice and corruption in our Court; certainly, they are the most cunning who have pressed nearest the throne! These fatted oxen will fare rarely hard now, they will! You should have seen the olden times— when I was young and called out to join the Colours;

when the Royal Standard, now in the Castle Armoury, was unfurled, and the King mounted his fine parade horse: it led the van, its long saddlecloth embroidered with crowns in the four corners: and then, in our fine galliard coats we formed up, while bugles began to call—calling and calling. . . ."

Again he took up the net and sought to weave, but soon threw it from him. He got upon his feet.

"Aye, Axel Friedrich, you should only have seen it all! Even in the moonlight, when we were drawn up in the snow, and began to sing psalms before the onset, I recognised the red and white of the Nerkingers, who looked liked striped tulips, and the yellow Kronobergar, and the lads in gray from Kalmar, and the merry Dal-regiment in blue, and the Westgöthens, who wore yellow and black. It was a pleasure to look at them all; and every one, too, as still as in the house of God. No, no! Nowadays, there's a different race of men altogether! Different uniforms, too!" And silence fell in the room.

Axel broke out with, "If my uniform and arms were in good order, perhaps, I would have some merry times . . . ?"

The old man shook his head.

"You are much too ailing; and then, there will be the heavy long marches, through the whole country down to the sea; and then over into Denmark."

"Yes, but I would not go in that fashion. Could I not take Elias and the long wagon with me?"

"Of course, we would allow you; but you have no

tent, with poles, and pegs, and rings, and things necessary."

"Elias could buy them for me, on the way down. The uniform, I can get together, I think."

"We will see. We will see just now!"

The old man grew eager. Hobbling over to the clothes press, he opened it.

"Ulrica, come here. Quick, Ulrica! Read out the Order, lying on the table, there, just as it is written by His Majesty," and he bowed. "Here we have the cloak with the brass buttons, lined with plain Swedish woollen. It is right; and the waistcoat, also. Read about the coat, now."

Ulrica snuffed the tallow candle. She seated herself beside the table. With her hands folded upon her brows she began to read aloud, slowly and monotonously.

"The coat, of blue unpressed cloth, the collar red with lining of madder-red woollen, twelve brass buttons down the front, four above and three under the flaps of the pockets, one button on the face of each pocket, and three small buttons on each arm.

"Eight . . . twelve . . . right. Now come the breeches.

"Breeches, of strong goat or deerskin, three buttons on the same, covered with chamois leather."

"These, here, are worn thin with riding; there will soon be holes in the seat of them. But Elias can try and get you a new pair, on the way. And now, the hat and gloves. Where are they?"

" They are in the chest, above the store-room,"
Axel Friedrich answered.

Ulrica continued: " Gloves, with large gauntlets of
yellow neats' skin, strong, thick, and chamois-dressed,
the palms to be of good goats' leather. Boots, of
sound Swedish waxed leather, with strap cut out of
one entire piece: the sole, one binding sole, together
with one middle sole. The buckles, of brass."

" The boots are here and in fair condition. You
can get my spurs. Now, you should be a fine
Swedish soldier, I tell you, my lad ! "

" Neckcloth, of black Swedish woollen crape, one
quarter long and nine good inches broad, with a half
yard of Parduan ribands, two white, at both ends."

" Elias must buy these for you in Örebo."

" Pistols, two pairs. Holster, of black leather, with
flaps lined with napped woollen."

" You can have mine; and my broadsword is in
right preservation, too, with its sheath of calf's skin
and hilt of elk's. Thus should a Swedish warrior be
fitted for the fight. But now we must be thinking
about supplies for Elias, and getting ready the knap-
sack and things appertaining."

Axel arose, and stretched himself. Said he, " It
will be for the best if I get abed, so that I can rise
betimes."

Throughout the whole house now began a bustle
and running about; every one was busy. All day
long there went on a rapping, and a hammering,
and in the kitchen stewing and baking. At night
candles were lit, and work was continued. The only

room in which reigned darkness was Axel Friedrich's. On the last evening of all no one went to bed save him.

When day dawned and lights were to be extinguished, his aunts awoke him. They brought him, too, a warm drink and cordial drops, having heard him coughing much during the night.

When he came downstairs every one was already gathered; the table was common to all. They eat in silence. When the meal was ended every one stood up: the Bible was put before his grandfather at the top of the board; and Ulrica, in a choking voice, read aloud the Sacred Writ.

When she had finished, the old man folded his hands. With closed eyes, he prayed:

" Even as my fathers have done before me, so will I now in the hour of thy departure lay my hands on thee, on thee, my daughter's son, and bless thee ; for my years are many, and who knoweth when my time is at hand. To God the Almighty I pray, in the dust I pray, that He lead you to glory, and that the heavy trials awaiting us all may exalt our little people into one great and God-fearing."

At the table-edge Axel was standing, pressing his thumbs on a plate; noisily it tilted upward. From without there echoed in the loud rattling of the long wagon, as it drew up before the door.

All crowded outside. Snugly wrapped in his grandfather's wolfskin, for with the continued thaw wet was falling from roof and tree, Axel Friedrich seated himself beside Elias.

"Here is the butter tub," said his aunts, "and the breadsack. Elias, put them in. The great cheese is in the wagon-box, and the flask of cordial. Now, dear Axel Friedrich, when the fatigues and hazards get too great for you, never forget the road home is aye open!"

But the old man pressed forward between them, and thrust his hand into the wagon.

"Is that box well tied down, now? And let me see: here are the brushes, the towels and combs . . . and here we have the haversack and flask. Everything is as it should be—the casting mould, the shears, and the casting ladle are all in the chest, there. . . ."

Ulrica stood behind him, unnoticed by any. Softly she cried:

"Axel Friedrich, when summer comes in, I'll go out of a night and tie the Thread of Joy and the Thread of Sorrow on the rye; and next morning will see which is waxed the greater. . . ."

"Everything is right, now!" the old man interrupted with, not hearing her. "God be with you and Elias."

But, just in the very instant of departing, when Elias was raising his whip, Axel laid a hand on the reins.

"Maybe this journey will have a bad ending," said he.

"It would seem so in any case," answered Elias, "and the more if we unyoked now, and later on were to start again."

Akel Friedrich put his hand up the cuff of his furs again, and through the rows of mute women and bondmen and labourers the wagon rolled away. . .

The weeks passed, and trees began to burst into green.   Weary was the journey in pursuit of the Nerikesen regiment through depopulated Sweden. Beside Elias, Axel sat, mostly sleeping ; his faculties all in a whirl.   On his hands he was now wearing mittens of soft goats' hair.   Then a good way out of Landskrona the wagon got among the baggage of the army : and the horse stood at ease in the sun and browsed along the ditch side.   Master and man fell asleep, shoulder to shoulder.

The horse kicked out at the flies, and the water trickled along the ditch bottoms ; two vagrants abused the sleepers ; but still they remained in undisturbed and tranquil slumber.   Then a rider came galloping furiously behind them.   Plainly clad was he, and wore a great yellow periwig.   When close upon the wagon he checked his chestnut.

Elias jogged Axel in the side, and pulled on his reins.   The young master would not open his eyes.

" Yes, yes," he murmured, " drive on.   I need all the rest against the coming fatigues."

Elias jogged him again.   " Rouse up, rouse up," he whispered.

Then Axel unclosed a drowsy eye.   The next moment he had jumped up, his face flushing hotly, and saluted.   It was the King, whom he had straightway recognised, from pictures of him.   Yet he had imagined a person entirely different.   Was this tall, self-conscious, somewhat stately looking young man he who only a few months previous had been beheading calves and goats, and breaking windows? He was not over middle-height; was small of face, but with brows high and noble; and from his full, deep-blue eyes shot persuasive glances.

"Sir, you must take off these furs, so that I can inspect your uniform," said he in a measured voice. "Everything seems to go well." Axel groaned within himself, and stripped off the old man's wolfskin.

The King examined the coat and buttons, poked and fingered about them. He examined everything.

"Fair," cried he, in a voice weighted with precocious gravity. "Ah, now we all should be wholly new men!"

Axel stood still, heavy with sleep but erect. His eyes were fixed hard on the wagon wheel. The King slowly added:

"A few days hence, maybe, we have the fortune to face the enemy. I have been told that in a fight nothing afflicts one so sore as drouth. So, if ye should meet me in the brawl, come forward and pass me your flask." And putting spurs to his horse, he set off again.

Axel Friedrich sat down. He had not formed impressions either of affection or hatred, nor had he experienced fear or delight; but the words of the King he kept turning over in his mind. And the furskin remained lying between him and Elias.

When the wagon rattled into Landskrona, tents were already pitched. Axel look about for the fine

arrays and carousings concerning which he had oft-
times dreamed : he found only sad-visaged comrades,
who but wrung his hand, and stood together in
groups, staring over the Sound. There the waves
surged wild beneath lowering heavens, and flags and
pennants streamed multitudinous above the forests of
masts.

Elias took the precaution of hiding the horse and
wagon in a barn, for the Crown had pressed all conveyances. Four and twenty hours after the fleet
sailed, he was to follow in a fishing boat, and land in
Zealand.

He was standing on the shore, at the edge of the
water, when the quaint anchors dripping sludge were
hove up with cables and windlasses acreaking. Swel-
ling canvas crowded yard after yard ; and the sun-
beams sparkled on the high lanterns and quarters of the
ships ; and the swell in glittering sallies made the tall-
sided vessels dance and cluster and gambol about, as,
bedecked with laurel and tridents for the victory, they
were wafted towards distant unacquainted lands, towards adventure and the deeds of heroes.

By now the massy vapour hung low down the
horizon, the sky was clear, and the air azure as ever
in a fairy tale. The King, who was standing in the
stern of his ship, close by its lantern, clean forgot himself ; the child in him conquered ; he clapped his
hands for very joy. About him the grey-headed
warriors of his father's time laughed and likewise
began clapping. Even His Excellency Piper, the
Count, leapt up the hatchway, nimble as a seaman.

Here was no senility and sickliness, no self-seeking wranglers; the host was the host of youth. Then, as at a signal all trumpets and bugles pealed, swords flew out of scabbards, and, the Admiral's order ringing wide, a psalm arose out of the nineteen ships of war and their smaller craft, from thousands of throats.

Elias discerned his young master again; he was wedged among gabions, earthbags, and Spanish horse, and sitting on his grandfather's wolfskin. He also noted how tardy Axel arose and drew the sword like his fellows.

After he had watched the fleet slowly disappear, he went back to the barn. He passed his hand over his eyes, and shook his head. He muttered, " How will he manage to look after himself, in his ill-health, till I come up with him ? "

.   .   .   .

Some days after this Elias once more journeyed with his wagon through Smaaland. The peasant wives recalling him to be the man who had travelled by with the officer slumbering at his side, opened their door halfway, and asked him if it was true that the Swedes were landed in Zealand, and that the King, when on bended knee to thank God for the victory, had stammered in sad confusion. He only nodded in reply.

Day after day, step by step, he went up into the North. All the time he trudged, reins in hand, along- side the conveyance, over which a piece of canvas was spread. And at last he approached the garden beside the homestead.

Everyone knew by the noise that it was the wagon. All in consternation they ran to the windows; the grandfather, himself, came out upon the steps; Ulrica stood midway in the courtyard. But Elias never hurried.

At the steps the horse came to a stand of its own accord. Elias carefully drew aside the canvas. A long, narrow, rough-hewn coffin of deal lay there, a withered wreath of beechen leaves upon its lid.

" I brought him home," said Elias. " The bullet hit him in the breast as he was springing forward to the King, and passing him the flask."

CHAPTER V.

GUNNEL, THE KEEPER OF THE CASTLE STORES.

In a dwelling within the fortress of Riga, Gunnel sat spinning. Eighty years old was she. Her long arms were sinewy, their veins outstanding; thin and flat was her bosom, like to that of a man; a few scanty locks of white hair hung loose over her eyes. She wore about her head a cloth resembling a round cap.

As her spinning wheel whirred, a young trumpeter lying on the stone flags before the fire spoke out.

" Grandmother," said he, " can ye not sing something as ye spin? Never yet have I heard aught from you but scolding and wrangling!"

She turned her tired, crafty, lack-lustre eyes on him.

" Sing. Maybe of your mother? they put her into a cart and sent her over to the Muscovites. Of your father, eh? strung up in the chimney of the brewhouse. I will curse the night I was born; curse myself and every man I meet. Tell me of a single person who is not worse than he is said to be!"

" Grandmother, sing a song; ye would grow cheerful. Fain would I see ye cheerful this night."

F

" Aye, when one sees a person laughing and making sport, 'tis but because he knows how to cozen. It is all shame and starvation with us; it is for our sins and debauchery the Saxons are lying before the town. Hear to the cannon? how they crack and roar! But why are ye not on the ramparts, doing duty with the rest, instead of sitting lazily in doors?"

" Can ye not say one kind word to me, grandmother, afore I go out?"

" I would thrash ye instead, but am too frail now! Ay, so bowed down with years am I, that I can never again lift my eyes skyward. Will ye have the truth? Do not folk call me the soothsayer? What if I should say then, that the slanting line above your eyebrows tells of a sudden death. I read the ages to come, see into them for a time and a time; yet with all my far vision I perceive nought only wickedness and baseness. You are worse than I am; I am worse than my mother was; and all those born will become worse than those who die."

He arose, and put the fire-wood in order.

" I will tell, grandmother, why I am here to-night, and am asking for a kind word. The old Governor-General has given order this day, that on the night after this all our women, young and old, sick and strong, are to be thrust without the gates, so that there be bread for us men. How can ye endure tramping about in the winter cold through field and forest? In the last ten years ye have been no further than across the courtyard to the store rooms!"

She laughed. Faster and faster she whirled the

spinning wheel. "Ha! ha! I have expected it, for all I have so faithfully kept our great lord's store-rooms, and everything that was his. And you, Jan? Ye are troubled, because there will be nobody now to make up the bed on the sleeping shelf, and cook and bake? Are there any thoughts but these in the minds of the young? Yet, glory be to God, God, who in the end throws us all under the scourge of His Anger."

Jan folded his hands round his curly brown hair.

"Grandmother! grandmother!"

"Go, I say. Let me sit in peace and spin my flax till I open the door and creep out to that spot where I shall lose my earthly life."

He worked the distaff for a little, then of a sudden turned round and went out. She whirled and whirled the spinning wheel, till the fire was burnt out. . . In the morning, when Jan returned, the dwelling was empty.

The siege was now become fierce and lengthy.

Accordingly, after divine service, all the womenfolk were turned out into that snowy day of February, the weak and ailing being put on wagons, and barrows, and stretchers. Riga became a throng of men who had not bite nor sup to give the hordes of women begging piteously for meat, as they skulked at the base of the city walls; there was scarce enough for the defenders themselves. In the stables hunger-maddened horses tore at each other, crunched their bits, or gnawed great holes in the sides of the stalls. Smoke hung thick over the fired suburbs. Often were the garrison aroused by the alarm bells to out and draw the sword.

When the trumpeter returned that evening, he found his bread already made up, and a dish of mouldy victuals on a stool. He was ashamed to tell anyone about this; he feared that his grandmother lay smothered deep in a snow wreath, and now was haunting his vicinity, in repentance of her hard-heartedness. After he had strengthened himself in prayer he grew calmer.

But as time passed he became more troubled and afraid. Occasionally he found the bed unmade, and no platter on the stool. So he must needs busy himself at the spinning wheel; and softly treading it, listened with growing reassurance to the well-known sound; from his birth had he listened to it.

Now it came one morning that Eric Dahlberg, the Governor-General, of seventy-five years fame, heard a sudden outburst of musketry. In haste and irritation he got up from his plans and waxen model of the fortifications. . . As a recollection of the joyous incursions of his younger days into the realm of beauty, there hung on the walls of his room numerous magnificent engravings of the ruins of Rome. But now his features, formerly mild and beneficent, wore a cast of sombre, brooding thought; a line of sternness curved about his small, well-nigh colourless lips, now close-knit.

He pulled his full-bottomed wig straight, stroked his thin moustache with a shaky finger, and stepped out into the staircase. He struck his stick hard against a step.

"Ah, we Swedes," he muttered, "we kinsmen of the Vasa Kings, who can but curse and accuse in their old age, and in the end are afraid of themselves in the dark of their own chambers, black seed lies sown in our souls. With years, a vast outspreading tree will shoot up from it, full of the bitterest of gall-nuts."

As he descended, his mood became the harder and more acerb, until, when he stood upon the ramparts he would speak to no person.

A battalion had formed up, with colours flying and drums a-rub-dubbing. But the venture was over by now ; already loose bands of the tired and wounded were filing through the gateway. Rearmost, came a very meagre and exhausted ancient. A ruddy sabre cut gaped in his chest, yet with strenuous exertion he was trailing home a dead boy lying in his arms.

Eric Dahlberg shaded his eyes with his hands, to see the better. Was it not Jan, the trumpeter, the lad from the fort overhead ?

The exhausted soldier sank down on a low mullion in the vaulted archway. Here he remained, his wound guttering, the dead upon his knee. Troopers bent over him to examine his wound ; and the bloody shirt over his bosom was slit open.

"What !" cried they, starting back. "It is a woman !"

In acute surprise they leant down, and scrutinised her face. Her head was now sunk against the wall ;

the fur cap was fallen to one side ; locks of white hair were revealed.

" She is Gunnel, the Stewardess," they ejaculated.

She breathed heavily. Her dimming eyes unclosed. She panted :

" I did not want to leave my bairn alone in this evil world ; but I put on a man's clothes ; and day and night have done my work with the others. I thought I had a right, then, to eat the soldiers' bread."

The officers and men look irresolutely at the Governor-General, whose decree she had broken. He was standing there, gloomy, sinister, reserved as ever.

The stick shook in his hand, and fell on the flagging. Slowly he turned round to the battalion. His lips moved apart.

" Dip the colours," said he.

CHAPTER VI.

MAANS THE FRENCHMAN.

A LEATHERN-COVERED army wagon was stuck fast in a Polish marsh; its horses were already being unyoked. On the wagon stood a young man, who a little while previous had joined the forces, in an endeavour to better himself. Maans the Frenchman, his comrades had nicknamed him, inasmuch as on his accompanying a distinguished young nobleman to Frankfort, as tutor, he had stuffed his baggage with all kinds of fine apparel. Near by, Olof Oxehufvud the Captain, and his officers and men, were tarrying for him. The snow was beating heavily against their faces.

Cried Oxehufvud, " The wagon and baggage must needs stay here."

Maans, opening his things, began to take out as much as he could carry.

"What a rare dressing-gown, with lace and tassels!" exclaimed the Captain and his officers. "What fine slippers!"

" And note, too, the false calves for his legs!"

" Aye, and the hats, there."

" It is a cadeau of my mo——"

" Away with it, into the snow!"

" —— of my mother's."

"See, the little perukes, there, and the great full-bottom, too!"

Oxehufvud could no longer contain himself. He laid hold of Maans.

" Into the snow, with one and all, I say!"

Maans' jocund, somewhat delicate-looking face flamed red. He drew his sword. Cried he:

" Captain, so wor——"

" So worthy a personage can easily retard our march, you mean?"

"No! So worthy and victorious an army, I thought to say, must not go clad of a night in dressing-gowns, old as the days of ' King Orres.'"

" Madman! Petit-maitre! Thickest of simple-tons!"

" You treat me as a mere slave, Captain! I have had much experience, I tell you! Ay, through the whole of France I have travelled; and even stood eye-to-eye with the famous Vauban."

"Indeed! And what said Vauban?"

" What said he?"

" Yes!"

" ' Va t'en,' quoth he, for it was in his own door-way, and I was standing in his way."

"Is that so? Is that so? But down from the wagon with you at once. Quick! Once—twice—thrice. And two men of you, there, step forward to carry this little masterpiece in a gold chair."

Maans bundled up the slippers and perukes in the fine dressing-gown, threw the pack upon his back, and put his lorgnette to his eyes; then he trudged forward.

On arriving on sound ground Oxehufvud came close to him   Long and lanky was the Captain, with ruddy cheeks and a small black moustache.

" Will monsieur listen.   What does he think to do in particular in the field ?   Aught at all ?

"Although, I am not noble born, I trow so," cried Maans. " Who knows !   Maybe, some day, I will have a patent of nobility in my pocket ! "

" You can go to hottest hell, so far as I am concerned, with your nobility ! " the Captain replied. " Nothing is asked about that in this army.   Every one must serve as serve he can ! "

Oxehufvud, as superior officer, had now vented his irritation on Maans, and teased and tormented him in full.   The spirit of camaraderie arose in him.

" If monsieur carries himself brave enough," he growled something more amicably, " he can begin with me to win his right to the authority of an officer; already, we've given finishing touches to several Swedish coxcombs, of monsieur's kidney; made them into men of stuff.   Does monsieur see that white house behind the wood, there.   At that spot he will take up his post, till I send further orders ; the rest of us station ourselves one-quarter mile further in the forest.   We are but twenty-five all told, so I cannot give monsieur a single man.   Now, keep alert and your eyes quick, for fear the enemy fall upon our rear."

Oxehufvud drew away with his little troop; and Maans turned to the dwelling, his bundle on his back. Not a person was to be seen.   Irresolutely he took shelter behind the wall of the house. Nigh frozen was he, wet to the skin, and yet what troubled him most was the dirt and soil bemiring his boots. Could he not keep a wary outlook from a window? And he longed too for a sweet-smelling bed, with silken eider-down and snug foot-muff.

A shed slanted out from the side of the house, and thither he went, skirting the wall with great circum-spection. He wiped the moisture off his lorgnette, put it to his eyes, and, bending forward, peered into the darkness of the shed. Something began to rustle and stamp about. The next instant he saw two glowing eyes. With his heart clappering, he jumped back, and drew his sword. A black horse dashed out into the court-yard, and wildly careered hither and thither, scattering the snow with its hoofs.

I had better not seize that mad beast, thought Maans. When a trooper mounts a brute like that, its dead owner rises out of the marsh, and leaps on behind him, and tears him out of the saddle. Aye, one hears the tale every night round the camp fires!

Menacing the horse with his sword, he stepped inside. The wings of the door in the opposite side he shoved apart; and his neighbourhood became much more distinct. It was observable, that the door of the house was built up. Snorting and trampling, the brute returned on him; but Maans jagged it with his blade, and drove it away. Then he went out and round to the front of the dwelling, and shouted valiantly.

A gray-haired serving-maid put her head out at a window.

"Whoever lives here, is he for King Stanislaus, or the Saxon drunkards?" cried he.

"An old solitary lives here, who is an enemy of no man! and has no man as his enemy!"

"Good! Then he will not refuse shelter to a half-frozen Swedish soldier?" Maans, cried anxiously.

The woman disappeared. In some little time she came back with a ladder, up which he scrambled into the house. The room was spacious; and plain, but well-scrubbed chairs stood along the bare untapestried walls. When by chance his scabbard struck against one of the seats, the maid hastily pulled him in place again. Before him two girls came and went without speaking. Theirs were fair features and curling tresses. Whenever one of the twain lagged behind, she hurried again in all anxiety to her sister; they kept close to each other; and, notwithstanding the daylight still held, bore two flaming lamps before them. When the serving-maid was finished brushing the dirt from his boots, and cleansing the floor of his dirty footprints, she opened the door of a neighbouring room, noiselessly and with caution. Said she, in a whisper, "Step in lightly."

Within stood a middle-aged man, wearing a dressing-gown. His was the sharpest and most impertinent nose ever imaginable. Never before had man worn such a finely curled and bepowdered wig. His fingers sparkled with rarely-jewelled rings.

Maans set his bundle down and eyed him through

his lorgnette. Much contented with his restored appearance, he gave a salutation with his arms, and bowed low.

"Sir, I am present on no rogue's errand," cried he. "In all humility do I ask the favour of knowing to what nobleman I have the happiness to address myself?"

"Be seated, sir. I would you be seated! I am nothing more than an old and forgotten recluse. But you, sir, appear to be a man of quality; thus will I explain to you what possibly seems so singular." With all necessary punctilios both seated themselves, their hands upon their knees.

"Once-a-day I was a gay man of the world," said the recluse, "and all Varszava talked about my clothes. But when my thirtieth birthday came round, and I sat making merry with my boon companions, I lifted up my goblet. Said I, as if fortuitously: 'My friends, with every year that passes, the eye grows harder and the heart chills. The one, here, is for King Stanislaus with the white cheeks, and the other, there, for King Augustus with his great paunch; and accordingly both of you intrigue and strive for high places and emoluments; now, I do not intend to descend to the grave with the melancholy recollection that each of my friends became in the end a Cain. I treasure friendship much higher than personal regard, for it paramountly binds soul and soul. Thus it is, I take my last farewell of you all, while we are yet young. Never again will you hear anything concerning me; and as I appear to you now, so will you aye be present

in my mind's eye; and thus will accompany me when
I am old and lonely; and when the serving-maid
hears me talking to myself,' 'There,' she will say,
'he is speaking with the dear companions of his
younger days!'"

"And then, after you had said farewell?"

"I came home, here, and bade them wall up the
door; the servant folks can get in and out as best
they can."

"Ah! Happy the guest of a host filled with such
fine sentiments."

"Happy! you say. Both my twin daughters,
who perambulate the house, as you see, with
their lamps, are half-witted! their mother was an
abducted nun! . . . And yet, I have but told
the least. . . ."

"Perhaps, you mean that I disturb you?" Maans
cried hastily.

"No! I will not say that, but. . . . Do you
hear the ghost?" And the nostrils of the recluse
expanded; he stood rubbing his hands, in some hidden
enjoyment. "I think it is my duty to tell you the
truth! It is a dead lackey who haunts the house;
Jonathan is his name. Wearing a brown livery with
black braid on it, he lingers in the window-nooks and
hides behind doors. The iron of servitude is yet so
embedded in him, that when any guest appears
and needs the slightest service, he comes from the
dead, and must needs wait upon his desires. 'Tis
lucky for me, I have few guests! Tell me, are you a
count?"

" I? No!"

" Are you a baron?"

" No! I am not yet a baron."

" You are not a plain nobleman, even?"

Maans reddened in confusion. Cried he, " Do you think to insult me?"

Yet he thought, certainly the title is my dearest dream, and God grant that soon I may have it. Then no one durst call me ' Petit-maitre.' They will say, then, ' Oh, 'twas very plain, he would be made a noble some day.'

"Can such a simple question annoy you?" the solitary said, tickled with greater amusement than before.

" I am a noble, certainly!" replied Maans in haste. " My stock is ancient."

" Oh, all will be well, then," said the recluse. " Although Jonathan was given a Christian burial and all due ceremonies, yet he is not purged of earthly humours. He is such an inveterate attendant on right true aristocrats, that he is quite capable of all possible wickednesses when he realises he is attending a mere commoner or startling!"

Maans stroked his little moustache with his small finger-nail, and in uneasiness swung his lorgnette to and fro. At last, said he:

" My lord, are you a lover of Syracuse wine?"

" No!"

" I also prefer a tassie of Frontignac. My favourite dish is a ragout with mushrooms, yet I will not contemn a hash of mutton and thyme seasoning withal.

In this world, much depends on the sauce, too! I admit, when I am at home, I do not want sweets at all ; nor the dark of the night."

" The darkness? You are thinking on the summer evenings ? "

" Ah, they are clear enough."

" And the winter nights are likewise clear, for then thoro io tho cnow. But, if you aro afraid of tho darl;, never travel further south than this ! In your country, you will have great artists and scholars ? "

" We neither have them, nor do we need them," Maans answered.

" You do not over-value your countrymen, then ? " ejaculated the solitary.

" My lord," said Maans, " I have seen something of the world. For two whole months I have done nought but travel in France ; even seen Le Roi Soleil with these very eyes ! "

" You ? Have you seen Louis the Fourteenth ? "

" That I have," Maans replied proudly. " In the theatre . . . for all I had but the fewest inches of standing room in the pit, I saw him. Oh, since Augustus, never has such an august lived. Take at random just the method way with which he greets one."

" But the King of Sweden ? " the solitary cried ironically, " he is a man, also."

" He is," Maans asserted. " He has drawn all eyes abroad to look upon us. Yet, how poor he is ! "

" Poor, you mean ? But there, lately, in Vars-zava ?—when Stanislaus entered the Church of the Coronation, his Queen bashful and trembling as usual, and with the sceptre, the apple, the sword, the ermine, the girdle, and the shoes of your King; even the banner, and the hangings from the church walls, the table plate, and the Crown monies which soon got scattered abroad again! And then the troops were on the watch, and fired salvoes . . . and in the end he thanked and kissed His Excellency Piper's hand. But, are you yourself poor?"

"Poor? I!" And Maans recollected with misery his whole wealth, the two pieces of gold sewn into the hem of his coat. Yet he tapped carelessly on the table with his eyeglass.

"My means are quite unusual," he replied in some little hurry. "The play amuses me: seldom do I go out with less than ten louisd'ors in my purse."

"Will you lend me five?" the solitary asked all in a rap.

Maans looked up at the ceiling.

"Truth to tell, unfortunately I left my purse in my great coat hanging up in the tent. But I will take it upon me to send you the trifle at the first chance. Yet you must not imagine that we embarrassed Swedes, my lord, are grand seigneurs! And I?—However high I rise, Maans will aye be peering between the seams of my clothes."

"Embarrassed," ejaculated the solitary. "It was but lately, that on our own battle-fields, here, Arvid Horn sat, notebook in hand, putting down all those opposing the Swedish authority; and our Province-Marshall, here, broke his baton in despair! . . . Now, make yourself as easy in my house an it were your own. The tobacco pipe lies next to the smelling bottle, and the smelling bottle is on the powder box, and the powder box on the tobacco box, and the tobacco box lies on the night stool ; and it you had best seek speedily, for time goes quickly." So speaking, he took up a leathern-bound volume, and began to read.

" Thanks, thanks," Maans answered, looking some-thing askance at him with greatening mistrust. Yet he thought to himself : Wait, yet a little while, till I have my patent, then they will say, " That nobleman, there, is our new and gallant M. Magnus Gabriell."

Again the young women glided through the chamber, lightening the gloom with their lamps. Maans stood up, and bowed. When the recluse deep in reading, gave no attention to him, he picked up his bundle, and returned to the adjoining apartment.

" Time wears on, and it is getting dark," quoth he to the ancient serving woman. " I am too tired, to be company to him any longer ! "

" Your bed is ready ; to the left, here, in the great hall," she answered. " It is the only room heated against the night."

This apartment was lengthy, and painted white, with rows of inhospitable looking chairs arrayed along its wainscot, and containing two rough-made folding tables. Near the door stood a bed with curtains of hollands stuff.

The ancient lighted the four tapers in the candelabra, then left. Shivering somewhat, Maans looked about him. He laid his sword on the nearer table, and

G

began to unpack his bundle. Then three of the candles he blew out, and hung thereon his little, his larger, and his largest perukes; but with the fourth light he looked under the bed and in the window corners.

"Impertinent buck!" he muttered. "I had liefer I had stopped outside in the snow; but seeing that I have got inside, I needs keep watch. I'll go often to the window, and spy about and listen."

The door he endeavoured to secure from the inside, but there was neither bolt nor lock. After he had laboured in vain to slip off his wet boots, the smell from which annoyed him, he attired himself in his fine dressing-gown and laid him down on the bed.

Now and again he heard the hollow-sounding snorting and tramping of the horse beneath him, but in time all was still. The one candle was giving out an obscure illumination; all nooks and corners lay in deep darkness. To sharpen his sight, Maans picked up his lorgnette, and turned his eyes into every niche and cranny of the chamber, yet lying motionless.

On a sudden he perceived, close to the doorway at the head of the bed, a tall, stiffish lackey: his coat was of black cloth, trimmed with brown braid. Erect and still stood he there. A spasm of fear contracted Maans' throat; everything swam before his sight; yet thought he within himself, the good God sends this visitation for that I dream of high honours and nobility.

Noiseless and imperceptible to the lackey, he gripped the side of the bed with both hands to overmaster his shaking body. Then he thrust his right foot out between the hangings. Said he firmly :

" Jonathan, take off my boot."

The lackey grinned ; his mouth curved back to his ears ; but he did not move.

Maans' teeth started achittering ; yet he drew not back his limb.

" Jonathan ! is that how ye serve a noble?" The ghost but grinned the more portentous, and gave a disdainful motion of the hand.

Maans the Frenchman knew then that the lackey apprehended his lies ; it was as a startling, and gross commoner he was treating him. His terror swelled so great, that he groaned aloud. Yet, despite all, he maintained the outstretched limb.

" Pull off my boot, Jonathan ! " His voice now was but a whisper.

The ghost made a despicable motion of his hips, and, grinning the more, remained stockstill. At the same moment the beast below neighed long and shrilly, and from out the distance other horses replied. Maans leapt from the bed.

" I forget my duty," cried he. " It is the enemy ! "

He dashed forward for his sword ; but with long steps the lackey came instantly beside him, and stared into his eyes : Maans' strength went from him ; he stood there like one charmed ; and the lackey was seizing the sword with one hand while with the other he reached up to the candelabra. Lifting down the largest peruke with two fingers, he extinguished the remaining light.

G—2

"Lord God," stammered Maans. "I have gone but seldom into Thy house, and have sinned and done all sorts of wickedness; but Thou help me in this hour, that I do not neglect my duty, and get shame; then afterwards punish me for all eternity."

The nickering of steeds grew louder and louder; and the horse below in the shed continued its fierce stamping and snorting. Maans clenched both hands over his head, and launched himself through the darkness upon the lackey.

"Thou spark of Beelzebub!" he shouted.

He tore the sword away from him, and beat about with it on all sides; chairs fell hither and thither. Never he laid a hand on Jonathan. Then his fists knocked against the wall, and the door flew open. There appeared the twin sisters with their lamps; with nothing on save their white linen shifts, being too ignorant to be ashamed; and clinging close to each other. Wide-eyed they stared at the stranger, who had awakened them with his hurly-burly.

Maans gave himself no time for courteous airs. He threw up the window, and jumped to the ground. In dressing-gown, and sword in his fist he took to his heels. He heard a raucous voice behind him; but knew not if it came from the solitary, or Jonathan, or both.

"I saw at once ye were a fool," it cried, "a prodigious fool; and wished to rid me of you! The troops have cast their eye on you now; you will be fighting hand-to-hand, in a little; and my house, my house, my refuge from the world, will be a heap of ashes before cock-crow."

Maans never looked round, but ran on among the trees. His sole thought was: now is the promise of my becoming an officer. And then the patent. The patent!

The moonbeams pierced the thinning snow-storm; he saw the Poles with their waving aigrettes hurriedly riding about on all sides; one might have taken them for shadows of the night. When they came danger- ously near, he dived behind some coppice or tree trunk. At last he saw in the dimness a stockade. Covered with snow it was.

As he approached, a soldier, rising from behind its logs and tree-stems, challenged him.

" Who goes there ? " he asked in a whisper.

" God with us ! good comrades," Maans answered, and clambered into the little triangular breastwork.

" The enemy is at our heels."

" It is a fair time since I first heard the trampling of their horses," replied Oxehufvud in a low, cautious voice. " In the end, the best for us may be to get back and occupy that house."

" Captain, do not ask me to know the road ! I was received there as a guest, and thus am bounden to them. I would rather shoot myself ! "

" And how were you treated ? "

" As a very Excellency."

" Would you just . . . No, too late now ! Present, men, fire."

A swarm of Polish horse was galloping upon them,

The enemy thrust their lances over the breastwork, at the Swedes ; but the first discharge emptied their saddles.

" Oh-a-haa.   Oh-a-haa."   The call re-echoed in the forest.   And shadowy dragoons and ranks of infantry surrounded them, far as the eye carried.   The dim spectacle was like to nothing else than multitudinous dark bushes slowly motioned by the wind.

" I think this will be a good brush with the enemy!" said Oxehufvud. " We are five and twenty men, and they are almost three battalions."

" Now we are only four and twenty," replied Maans, snatching the piece from the dead man's hand.

" Now we are nineteen," cried Oxehufvud, after a little while.   For bullets pouring in on them were slaying man for man.

On the foe falling back, the Swedes reserved fire ; but when, allured by the pretence of devastation and the stark silence within the stockade, the Poles hurled themselves forward, they were received with bullets and swords, and stones, and tree branches.   Hour after hour the defence was continued.

Oxehufvud looked about.   Half-aloud he counted. " Eight, nine, thirteen. . . Now we are thirteen. A bad number."   He also had seized a musket, and was at present bending down for ammunition out of a dead man's cartouche.

" Comrade," said he, without rising ; and he plucked at Maans' dressing-gown. " I treated you badly to-day in the marsh."

Maans only said, " We are seven now ; " and re-
loaded and fired. " We will have held out for some
three hours."

" You are not the first to show that we Swedes
are not always right in laughing at our young coxcombs. Mind you, sometimes it happens that what
begins with a noble periwig ends with a noble
deed ! "

" Now we are but two."

" Barely two, for I am already done," replied Oxehufvud, sinking back, " Not two."

Now among the dead Maans was standing alone.
He tore the dressing-gown off his body, and wrapped
a strip round his left arm, which was bleeding freely.
Likewise his vest he threw away. The lorgnette he
shoved into the leg of his boat. Then he lay down
among the others, creeping as much as possible under
the branches and trees of the breastwork. The Poles
whirled down again ; but all was still silent. With a
wild shout they crowded over ; and the plundering
began ; but seeing Maans, half naked, motionless, and
all bloody, they left him undisturbed. At the gray of
the morning their forces withdrew.

Now, thought Maans, now I come into my authority ;
the patent will follow later. And he crept out and
away.

Near the house he found his perukes in the snow,
for they had been thrown out after him.

" The wretch ! " he muttered. " This is all the
thanks for my having saved his nest for him."

All that day he held on through the forest, perukes

under his arm. It was late in the night when the outposts challenged him.

The tents and huts of the Swedes were standing in the open, unfortified. On the field wagons or before their huts, set apart in a section of their own, the women hushed their babes or conversed lightsome and merrily in undertones with their men. Round the camp fires the bowls of clay pipes glowed in scarred hands. There Braakenhjelm, cornet of horse, and the intrepid Lieutenant Pistol took account of their adventures. Lieutenant Örbom let them feel with their fingers the bullet of Klissov, still behind the left ear, having passed in under the left eye and through his head. Per Adlerfelt, the dancing master, made moan that the enemy, aye, aimed so low, even as recently at Düna; his shapely limbs were still suffering. Here, jested the audacious Dumky, who yet wore on his arm the garter stolen by him from a little Silesian duchess; Svante Horn linked to his trusty Lidbom, was saying that he could never fight well until he felt a Cossack spear or sword flesh him; and in front of him stood Field-surgeon Teuffenweiser, that courteous, whiteheaded old man, who was continually putting on and taking off his glasses. It was he who aye wanted a dram before he would attend wealthy patients.

All were talking about the chances in war; how that some were allowed to grow expert in danger and old in honour, without being grazed even by a bullet, and others, in the spring of life, were cut down at the very first shot of all. Not an echo of carousal was in the air ; but the King had ordered the drums and flutes to play merry-ways the whole night long. This was a camp wherein the subdued bustle sounded like the murmuring of a clear forest-stream under the leaves of June.

It had been against the King's desire that his Life Guards had thatched his tent with straw, and laid turf thereon, so that it resembled nothing so much as a pile of charcoal. It was not pitched in the centre but was the very last of the tents, and almost outside the firelight. They had put together a fireplace of stones beside the tent pole, and from time to time laid in it red-hot cannon-ball.

The King's laver was of pure silver. On the table there lay, next to " The Life of Alexander the Great," and the Bible garnished with covers of gold, a small silver cast of his dog Pompey, now dead. Already faded was the once bright blue silk of the seats and the bed wherein the dogs Turk and Snushane were lying ; the King himself was sleeping on pine boughs strewn on the ground.

By now even small beer was lacking in the commissariat ; Huliman, his body servant, had been able to proffer nothing more than a tassie of snow-water and two hard biscuits. Then the King had spread his cloak around about him, and put on his nightcap. There, in the height of his triumph, slumbered Sweden's King—his shapely head in the glare of the ruddy cannon-shot. Long past was the time since he had uttered in his privy chamber that prayer of childhood, while the night wind rustled the lime trees in Karlberg Park. Little by little his Deity had darkened into the God of wrath of the Old Testament; then changed into the vengeful Lord of Hosts, whose commands he heard echoing in his soul without any hearkening on his part; and now Thor and the Aesir Gods were storming upon his camp in the bellowing blasts of the night wind, greeting on trumps their youngest-born on earth.

The King's hounds began to growl. Max of Wurtemberg, the Little Prince, was approaching, all radiant and overjoyed. His voice rang like that of a child.

"Your Majesty! Waken, Your Majesty! Five and twenty Smaalanders have started and had sport with the enemy."

Maans stood behind him. Schmiedeberg, the mighty captain, supported him; he himself was yet going on crutches, after his stout affray about the baggage; there, with twelve men, he had engaged three hundred Poles. Maans had never borne his head prouder and more satisfied, although he was sinking with fatigue.

When he heard he was before the King's tent, he stopped in dismay, then stooped, and hurriedly washed the blood-stains from his hands. He threw off his hat, his large peruke, and the small one; and without recollecting the regulations, put on his great full-bottom. His toilette ended, with arms stiff by his sides he stepped into the tent. Through stuttering lips and with chittering teeth he gave his account to the King.

Charles, sitting upon his bed of pine branches, repeated every word of it to himself, slowly and with emphasis; not to let slip the meanest detail. He rejoiced and made glad, like a child concerning a tale of wonder. At the end he gave his hand to Maans.

" Oxehufvud was right," said he, " our men have had a merry brush with the enemy! Since the solitary asked in jest for five louisd'ors, I will pay out ten; and you, my man, can go back and throw them through the window at him ! "

Maans stepped backward out of the tent; and Schmiedeberg took him round the waist, and carried him into the midst of the officers awaiting him in curiosity. Cornets were there, and lieutenants, and captains: his equals in years, but already holding higher rank.

" Maans the Frenchman ! " they murmured. " None of us, now, durst laugh any more about your lorgnette and perukes ! But what of the rank of officer and the patent ? The patent ? "

" Hush," said Schmiedeberg. " Rewards are for the mean. It is His Majesty's will that no reward is given. The King would rather have one fight and fall for the glory, and the glory only." And none there ventured to gainsay him.

He let the new protegé stand free, and hobbled on his crutches some feet nearer the fire. Said he softly:

" Saw ye not, saw ye not, how His Majesty himself gave him his hand, just as to an equal ! "

" I got my award, at that, for time and eternity," cried Maans the Frenchman.

Attired in his fine full-bottom and tattered clothes, he held himself prouder and more erect, his arms by his sides.   His mouth was trembling with the cold.

"And thy letters patent?" Schmiedeberg replied softly : "When ye fall in the fight."

CHAPTER VII.

QUEEN OF THE LAND-RAKERS.

THE bells of Narva Church Tower stormed out no more. Among the stones from the gaping ramparts lay the hacked and rifled bodies of the heroic Swedish defenders. The Russians had carried the day.

Some Cossacks had sewed a live cat within the belly of an inn-keeper, and were standing around their victim, yelling with laughter. But the colossal Tzar, Peter Alexievitch, was crushing his way through the thick of the soldiery, felling his own people down in an endeavour to repress outrage. From his own feats in the fight the right sleeve of his coat was soppy with blood up to its shoulder.

In time, one troop after another, wearied with the slaughter, gathered in the market-place and the churchyard. On the pretext that the church was defiled by unbelievers buried therein, they began to violate and rifle the graves. They raised the tomb-stones in the church with crowbars, and opened the graves outside it with spades; coffins were smashed in pieces, and thrown broadcast in confusion; the pillagers cast lots for the silver handles and case-bands. All day long the coffins of metal and wood, rusty and decayed, lay strewn in the streets previously deluged with boiling pitch and burning wood, cast by desperate inhabitants on the first melées, but now with gutters running deep in gore; and the hair of some of the dead was waxed so thick, that it had forced itself out between the chinks. A few of the corpses were embalmed, and thus well preserved, their flesh brown and withered; but for the most, yellowed and grinning skeletons lay amid their rotted and musty winding-sheets.

At the fall of the darkness, men slunk out and examined the name-plates, oft-times reading thereon the name of a near relation, or mother, or sister. They saw the body-riflers tear out fœtid remains and fling them into the river; but often, protected by the night, they succeeded in securing these last evidences of loved ones. Frequently during the darkness there was to be descried an old man or woman, with their children and servants, struggling laboriously and in timor to bear away some coffin.

A swarm of sacrilegious soldiers were bivouacked in a corner of the churchyard. What a pleasure it was to make a fire of bedsteads, mattresses, chairs, broken coffins, and everything that could be dragged together. High the sparks shot up, even to the eaves of the pastor's house. Some coffins stood piled up about the fire; the bottom was fallen out of the topmost one; and the deceased treasurer came to view, long and lanky, with a full-bottom still upon his head. He looked as if he was about to say, " Heavens! into what sort of company have I descended?"

" Haha! little father," yelled the troopers at him, while spreading their apples and onions to roast. " You also want to have something in your throat, eh?"

The firelight illumed the living-room of the pastor, and the sparks fell through its broken windows. In the room was one table, much cracked, and one chair. The pastor was seated thereon, his head in his hands.

His silvery hair fell on his shoulders, his snowy beard swept his chest. As an army chaplain he had experienced well-nigh most things in the heyday of his youth ; and never had he refused a beaker of good liquor ; yet, later in life, had served the Lord his God in joy and well-doing. A widower, he was ; and 'twas whispered that when a fair handmaid served in the pastor's house, he was wont from the very outset not to flee from temptation. His heart was as staunch as his body, which, as becomes a man of war, was still unbent by the stress of years ; he was bearing the calamities with more courage and equanimity than the others his fellows.

" Who knows! Maybe I will succeed," he muttered, rising up as if he had found the key to some intricate puzzle.

He arose and went out into the passage. Carefully he pulled some four or five rusty nails out of the panelling, hiding a small narrow secret place under the stairway, and shoved it aside.

" Come out, my child," he cried.

On no one obeying, his voice grew louder. " Come out, Lina! The other maids were bound hand and foot and taken away ; I hid you just at the right time. But it will soon be four and twenty hours since ; and one cannot live without meat and drink ! "

When, despite him, he was not obeyed yet, he thrust his head back in affront. Said he, in a rough, commanding voice:

" Why do ye not obey ? " Think ye there is any food in the house ? there is not so much as a pinch of salt, now ! And do ye know, too, ye must be smuggled out of the town ? If things go amiss, and a soldier seizes you, then, dear child, I give but this advice : put your arms round his neck, mount behind him, and ride off with him whithersoever he takes you. Ay, often in the broils of my younger days I have seen that done ; even I have thrown my roque-laure over the pastor's frock ; and had a hand in a like affair before the happy conclusion to it all. Are ye listening, my girl ? When that father of yours— drunkard he was, too, to tell the truth about him— who was my stable man, drew me out of the hole in the ice, I promised to care for his wife and child. And then, too, he was a Swede, like myself ! Have I not aye been a fatherly master to you ? or what has your Grace to object to? Have you clean forgone your understanding, or what ? "

At last something began to stir in the pitch-dark-ness of the recess. An elbow was shoved against the wall ; and with much effort Lina Andersdotter came out in her white shift, with naked feet, her brown

tresses streaming down her back, and wearing a torn
red jacket, lacking sleeves, but with an unharmed
body. The firelight poured through the window.
Huddling herself together, she pulled her shift down
between her knees. Yet her fresh, healthy face, with
its broad, open features, was as cheerful as if she
were arisen from sleep in the first grey light of a
winter's morning.

The old man's blood yet ran hot in his veins; but
at this particular moment he was entirely the friend
and father. Said he, stroking her naked shoulders
in a kindly manner:

" I did not know that anyone in my simple household had such over-weening modesty ! "

She looked up. "No!" was her answer. " It is
because I am so cold."

"Ay, that is believable," said he. " But I cannot give you any clothing. And every moment the
house may take fire. Yet, I myself may be able to
slip out unmolested, and have still a Riga rix-dollar
in my pocket; who asks questions about an old man.
But it is quite different with you, Lina !—I know well
the wild business that would ensue! I can think of
only one device to get you away in safety; yet durst
not tell you, you are sure to become too much afraid ! "

"Afraid? I am not !" she replied. " What is to
be done to me—will be done. And I am no better
than any of the others. Oh, if I was not so fright-
fully cold."

" Come, then, to the door; but do not take fright.
See, there, outside in the doorway, the villains have

placed a smallish, wooden coffin. It cannot be too weighty for me to carry, and mayhap you will find room in it. An ye have enough courage to lay down in it, perhaps I can smuggle you out of the town."

" I have the courage now," cried she.

Her teeth were chittering with the cold, her whole body was atremble. But she straightened herself, letting the shift hang short, and stepped forth into the doorway.

The pastor raised the damp lid that hung loose, and found nothing more in the rifled coffin than shavings and a brown blanket.

" That is just what I need," stuttered Lina Andersdotter, drawing it out.

Then she enveloped herself in it, and laid herself down, back on the shavings. The pastor bent over her. He put both hands on her shoulders, and peered into her frank eyes. She was between eighteen and nineteen years; her glossy braids of hair were smoothed back from the temples. It came into his head that not always had he looked upon her with as pure and fatherly eyes as he ought to have done, and as he himself had pretended; but now, he was doing it for a righteous end.

His long, white locks fell over his face, and down on her cheeks.

"May all go well with you, child," he cried earnestly. " I am old; it matters but little whether my life is taken ! In my time, I had part in many rogues' ploys and have done many wicked deeds; and towards the remission of my sins I would that I do some good act,"

He nodded several times to her, then straightened himself. Without, the brawling was growing louder.

He put on the lid, and jammed down the long screw-nails as best he could.   Thereupon he knelt down and passed a rope round the coffin ; with strong arms he lifted the heavy burden upon his shoulders, and with bowed back went staggering into the open.

" Look there," cried one of the band in the church-yard.

His nearest comrade silenced him. " Let the old dullard go on.   It is a pauper's coffin ! "

The sweat trickled down the pastor's brows ; back and arms ached exceedingly ; but, step for step, he drew forward through the empty street.   Now and again to get breath, he had to rest the coffin on the ground ; but even then he stood with one hand on its lid ; then in fear he again had to bestir himself and push on, or remain to get cut down by marauders.   Frequently he had to avoid the great wagons laden with men and women who were to be carried hundreds of miles into Russia, to populate the steppes.   The great Tzar was a sower, who measured not the crop he sowed.

When at last the old man neared the gates, and the guard stepped forward, he strained his last forces with the whole energy of deadly fear.   While with one hand he kept the coffin on his back, he took out his rix-dollar with the other.   He handed it to the soldier. The man nodded to him to pass without the gates. He tried to step forward, but could not, yet through the gateway plainly saw the free fields and shimmering river.   Of a sudden everything became dark to him.

In his helplessness, yet ever careful of his burden, he let the coffin slip gently to the ground. Then falling forward on his face, he died.

Soldiers sprang hither. They began calling and complaining, for the coffin could not remain there, in the gateway. Their officers, who had been sitting at cards inside the gatehouse, also made their appearance. One of them, in shape small and thin and weakling, with spectacles square in shape, and resembling more a writer than a soldier, took a lanthorn, and coming forward raised the lid of the coffin just a little with his scabbard. The first time, he hastily drew back his head and almost dropped the light ; but he bent down again, directing the illumination inside the coffin. He paused longer this occasion, and looked with more accurate attention. He began to stroke his face with his hand, as if to conceal some thought. Finally he took off his spectacles, and stood there, pondering. When he stooped the third time, he flashed the lanthorn full along the slight gap betwixt lid and shell ; there lay Lina Andersdotter, at peace, and blinking at him without knowing what had happened.

Quoth she, " I am hungry."

The officer put the light on the ground, and took a couple of steps up and down the gateway, his hands behind his back. Then a mischievous and brisk expression played on his stiff features.

All unnoticed by his comrades he took an apple from his pocket. Cautiously he slipped it into the coffin. Then cried he to his men :

"Here, you lads. Eight of you to carry this coffin to General Ogilvy. Give him my humble greetings, and tell him that this is a meagre gift from his servant Ivan Alexievitch. Other eight of you, the men, there, just returned from the fortifications, go behind, and blow the march of the regiment on the trumpets. A couple of men, also, are to go before, with lighted torches. Forward!"

The soldiers looked in amazement at each other, but obeyed. Amid much laughter they raised their burden upon their muskets. Two long poles plaited around with straw were found in a corner of the gate-house, lit at the lanthorn, and the procession set out towards the camp that lay without, in the fields. Merrily the trumpeters blew their blasts.

When they reached the camp, the escort formed up, in the torchlight, around the coffin. General Ogilvy, who had been sitting at meat, came out of his tent.

"Little father," said the spokesman of the men, "Ivan Alexievitch, our lieutenant, sends this present to thee in all humility."

Ogilvy paled somewhat. He bit his lips under the bushy, grey moustache. His features wore a stern expression, though at bottom he was full of kindness and beneficence.

"Is he a fool?" he thundered in feigned anger, for truth to tell he was now out of countenance like a startled schoolboy. "Put the coffin down, here, and break open its lid."

The men shoved their swords between the boards,

and the lid fell aside. Ogilvy gave one look, then burst into loud laughter. He laughed so much that he had to sit down; the soldiers laughed too; along the entire street of tents the merriment spread, till men stotted hither and thither, falling against and propping up one another, as if intoxicated. For in the coffin lay Lina, wide-eyed, and with the half-eaten apple in her hand. She was warm by now; her cheeks glowed pink like a doll's.

"By the Saints!" cried Ogilvy. "One sees no such wonder in the catacomb of St. Anthony himself. This is a kind of corpse which must be sent to the Tzar."

"By no means, your Excellency," said one of his officers. "Yesterday, I despatched two small, short-legged blondes to him; but his desires are all for slim, brown-haired women."

"No, indeed, if that is so," Ogilvy replied. With a gesture he turned towards Narva. "Greet, then Ivan Alexievitch from me, and say to him that if the coffin be sent back, his promotion ought to lay inside it! Hoho! my little darling!" And he chucked Lina Andersdotter under the chin.

Instantly she got up, seized him by the hair, and gave him a resounding box on the ear. She followed it up with another. But he did not evince the slightest embarrassment, and continued to laugh.

"I will have you, now," he cried, "I will! I'll make you Queen of Land-Rakers, my chick; and, as token, I give you this armlet with the turquoise clasp; some of our cleverest knaves stole it just now out of Count Horn's coffin in Narva." And on his shaking the bracelet off his wrist, Lina Andersdotter eagerly seized it.

A little time later that night she sat at table with General Ogilvy. Now was she dressed in a gown of figured stuff, made in the French mode, and wore a head-dress of fine lace. She had to eat her food with gloves on her hands, with their great, clumsy fingers; and the red skin of her wrists showed out between the fastenings.

" Haha! Haha! " yelled the generals. " Her hands, there, make more merriment than tankardfuls of Hungary wine! Fasten her girdle for her; catches us under the arms. No one here can look at her without killing himself with laughter."

She pilfered as much of the sweets as she could, and thus through her audacity Ogilvy needs keep his sword on high to ward the dishes. This displeased her somewhat, and she made grimaces. In all truth her appetite was not small; but on the contrary she would not drink; she took but one sip of wine, then spewed it out on the generals. Their oaths and worst terms of speech she immediately attained. And there she sat, blooming and merry.

The generals were choking with laughter. Cried they:

" Blow out the lights, so that we cannot see her. Oh, save us all! Oh! We are suffocating. Mademoiselle, perhaps smoking a pipe of tobacco may be one of your little pleasing traits ? "

" Why the devil can you not leave me in peace!" replied she.

Ogilvy was adroit enough to hold aloof, so that none might be able to turn the laugh against him.   None nudge him.   None pluck at his coat-tails and say, "Ah, little father, now you have a douse of cold water over that bald head of yours.   God bless you, little father, bless you aye, and your little disappointment too."

He always contrived to behave to her rather as the benevolent acquaintance than aught else.   In public he never sat so close to her, but that his hound could lay between them.   Nor did he take hold of her in public, if any one was nigh ; and, even in private, he did but very seldom ; for she was wont to smack his face.   Oft-times so hard did she hit, that the glove split, and out came her robust hand in all its yokel ruddiness.   Frequently she belaboured him with a good will, and jeered at none so much as him.   But he just laughed like the others.   And never aforetime had such rioting and brawling reigned in the camp.

Ogilvy often resolved to let her feel the weight of the knout, yet was he ashamed, for his officers would hear the affair through the thin covering of the tent.   Then they would form some idea regarding his non-success with the virgin.

" Ay, only wait ! " he muttered between his teeth. "We will be alone some day, soon ; between four walls and behind lock and key ! Only wait, Mademoiselle ! "

One day the generals cried to her : " You trail your dress on the ground.   We'll take hold of it for you ! Now ! Bless me ! Look there ! Just look, but merely take one peep ! "

" Carry it, then," said she. " But do it fair and
decently, and the better for you ! " Then the officers,
thronging about her, bore her train for her, both on
her going in to meat, and coming therefrom.

Now it came one night as they all sat drinking,
Lina Andersdotter among them, that an adjutant
entered, all perplexed and in irresolution. He stepped
up to General Ogilvy.

" Dare I venture to speak plainly to you, your
Excellency ? "

" Of course, my man," the general replied.

" And will you pardon me ? '

" On my word of honour. Only say what you
desire."

" The Tzar is on his way to the camp ? "

" That is all right enough. He is my noble
sovereign."

The adjutant nodded in the direction of Lina
Andersdotter. Quoth Ogilvy : " Only the slender
ones please the Tzar."

" Your Excellency. This last time, his taste is
changed."

" Good ! " cried Ogilvy, jumping up. " Call the
men to arms, then get me a three-horse conveyance."

The call was sounded. There was a soaring of
bugles and a blaring of trumpets ; wagons rumbled
about ; sharp orders and the trampling of the cavalry
filled the ear of night. The carousal instantly came
to an end.

Lina was placed in the wagon. A soldier sprang
up, lanthorn in hand, and seated himself next to the

peasant driver. The wench heard the latter ask in a
low voice for his directions. " To the Tzar," replied
the taciturn man of war, pointing with his thumb over
his shoulder at her.

The driver shuddered as if struck by a frosty blast.
He whipped the fiercer at his small shaggy horses ;
and, crying and beating at them, forced them into a
speedier gallop.

The lanthorn gleam glinted among the trees, and
over the burnt-down houses ; the wagon rattled and
rumbled and creaked along the stony highway ; and
Lina Andersdotter lay on her back, and looked up at
the stars. Where were they taking her ? What fate
awaited her ? She wondered and wondered on these
thoughts. Round her wrist still hung the armlet,
like to a talisman ; a pledge it was towards the ful-
filment of the General's strange prophecy. Queen of
Land-rakers. The term sounded so natural to her,
for all she had arrived at its meaning with much
difficulty.

For a while she fingered and tugged at the little
silver ornament. Then she rose up a little, and,
bending over, looked at the rough track in the lanthorn
illumination. With caution she trailed herself more
and more towards the end of the wagon, and, all
unseen, climbed over the back board, and let herself
slip feet first towards the ground. She wondered
whether, at the furious rate they were travelling, she
would break any of her limbs, and only remain laying
on the road exposed to more danger. The next
moment she lost her grip, and was being trailed along

the ground, to stumble, and fall heavily on the hard road.   The conveyance thundered on, and in a short time had disappeared into the distance, with its dancing light and galloping horses.   Lina got upon her feet, dried the blood off her cheeks, and took her way into the trackless forest.

Here she fell in with some refugees, who taking pity on her comely face, plucked her roots and berries, and followed her.   Soon she discovered a whole household of fugitives.   She straightway showed the strong hand, so that they durst not even touch so much as her clothes ; yet, in truth, among themselves they were always quarrelling and striking each other. At last, one day, she took service with the wife of a seaman, who intended to set sail for Dantzic.   But scarcely was the gloaming fallen, than the others also appeared and offered their hands.   Then the seaman sat in the moonlight, on the top of his cabin, and blew his shawm for joy.   So willing a crew he had never had, nor his wife so strong a servant.

Hardly were they on the sea, than Lina Andersdotter placed herself with folded arms beside the shipman, and her vagabonds laid down on their backs.   Merrily they all sang to the music of the shawm.

Said Lina to the man's wife :

" Think ye, I will scour and scrub your tubs ? "

" Beat her ! Beat her ! " the woman cried.   But her husband leant the closer to Lina Andersdotter, and continued playing.

Night and day the vessel floated onward, with flapping canvas   The seaman all the time blew on the shawm to please Lina. In the cabin below his wife sat and wept.

On arriving at Dantzic, the shipman put his shawm under his arm and slunk away, by night, with Lina Andersdotter and her companions. They understood by now that her end was to join the Swedish troops that were marching against the Poles.

When with her folk she came singing into the camp, and along to the section for the women, she found resentment and clamour active there. For twice four and twenty hours the camp followers had remained on their wagons, without food. The last provisions had been given up to the sutler, and were now divided among the soldiery.

Lina Andersdotter went up to the first corporal she saw. Putting her arms akimbo, she cried to him:

"Are ye not ashamed to let my women folk starve, when ye cannot do without them?"

"Your women folk," quoth the corporal. "And who may you be?"

She pointed to her armlet.

"I am Lina Andersdotter, Queen of the Land-rakers. Now take ye five men, and follow me."

The soldier looked at his captain, the foolhardy Jacob Elfsberg. Then he gazed first at Lina's pleasing face, and finally at his men, who already, musket in hand, stood round her. Her women folk had taken to themselves whips and cudgels. So when the flare of their fires flushed the night sky, the King, sharpened with curiosity, sprang into the saddle.

On the wild gang coming back with heavily laden

wagons, with oxen and sheep, the troops were jubilant.
Their shouts rang lusty and loud: " Long live King
Charles !   Long live Queen Caroline ! "

The women thronged so close upon the King, that
his lackeys had to fend them off.   Lina Andersdotter
stepped straight to him to receive the shake of his
hand.   But he had raised himself in his stirrups.
Over the heads of the surging women he cried to the
corporal and the five men ;

" Well done !   Rare good plunder ye've got, my
men."

From this hour forth she would hear no more the
King's name mentioned in her presence, but when
she met a man, be he general or private, belaboured
him to his face with the worst of words.   When
Bjorkmann, the young guardsman, already famous
from his heroic feats; offered his hand to her, in irony
she put her empty, tattered purse into his palm.   But
never was she more furious than when Mayerfelt, the
major general, rode past her, whistling merrily as he
cantered at the head of his dragoons, or when she
recognised the yellow-brown cheeks and raven-black
bobtail wig of Colonel Grothusen.   Yet if a poor
wounded lay on the road, she would give him the
very last drop in her water bottle, and put him upon
her wagon.

Frost and scars soon tanned her cheeks.   She
always sat on the top of her baggage wagon, and
with her whip controlled all the odd after-guard ;
the punks and wedded wives and thieving wretches
that streamed from east and west in the wake of the

army. When the glare of fires illumed the heavens at night, the troops knew that Queen Caroline was out on her foray.

Now after days and years were gone by, and after the pleasant winter quarters in Saxony, the army of the Swedes advanced into the Ukraine. The King commanded that all their women be left behind.

" He does it all to suit himself ! " murmured Lina Andersdotter, but she kept quite calm.

No sooner was the army arrived at the Berezina than the camp women broke out into clamouring, and weeping and wailing. They gathered round Lina Andersdotter's wagon, some wringing their hands, others holding up their little children.

"What will you do now ? " was the intense cry. " The troops are over the water, already ; and break down all the bridges. They have left us to the Cossacks."

There she sat, her whip in her lap, and wearing topboots like a man. On her wrist still sparkled the armlet with the turquoise clasp. The lamentation and blubbering of the deserted women increased. Out of the close-wagons, like to huge boxes, crept powdered and painted wantons, some in satin gowns and having gold chains around their necks. They crowded about her; on all sides she saw women, strangers to her, whom she had never set eyes on heretofore.

" Low drabs ! " she muttered. " I understand now what sort of smuggled goods the captains and lieutenants carried ;with them. What do you here, among

my poor folks. Ah, the whole lot of us, now, know
the worth of a man when his haversack is light of
provisions.

Still they all kept thronging on her. They plucked
at her garments, and besought her, as if she of herself could avert approaching doom.

She cried : " Is there not one who knows that
Psalm, ' What though I walk in Death's dark vale ? '
Sing it ! Sing it ! "

Some of them struck up the Psalm, in choking,
whimpering voices. But others fled down to the
river bank, and sought boats, and began to row
across ; each that had a husband or lover hoping to
be taken back and somehow concealed from authority's eye. It was all the lowest of the women,
those who never at any time belonged to one man,
who were standing now clustered around Lina
Andersdotter.

Among the bushes the Cossacks began to skulk
towards them.

Then Lina felt her heart grow faint, and she got
down from her seat.

" Poor, poor children," said she, stroking their
tender cheeks. " I will not leave ye ; but now ye
must, devil take me, pray God that he washes your
blood-red sins white and clean. I can say no more
to you than that ye shall shame men and die a proper
death."

She opened the covering of her wagon, and searched
among her spoils for some pikes and sabres. These
she gave to the women, and herself seized an empty

musket ; powder and shot she had none.   So there they stood in that ominous atmosphere, high upon the bank, with the ruddy sunlight streaming down.

When the other women saw from the water how the Cossacks rushed the baggage, and cut down their comrades, thinking they were men in disguise, they turned away the boats.

The Swedes sped from their ranks back to the river-side, and opened fire.   They cried, a thousand throats as one : "

" Long live King Charles.   Long live. . . No. 'Tis too late !   Look.   Look !   It is Queen Caroline, who, surrounded by harlots, is dying like a virgin, with the musket in her hand."

CHAPTER VIII.

MAZEPPA AND HIS EMISSARY.

In a bed-chamber, garnished with sumptuous furniture, stood a tester bed. Plumes waved upon its four
posts. Behind its half-drawn curtains lay a man upward of sixty years of age; the bed-covering he had
drawn up under his beard, and his long white hair lay
spread out. The entire forehead of him was hidden
under a medicated plaster. 'Twas Mazeppa.

On the carpet by the bed two medicinal phials were
strewn, and a few volumes of Latin and French poetry.
At the door a small, meagre-bodied priest was holding
a whispered conversation with two men in garbs of
green; messengers they were, from the Tzar.

"He scarce understands your words," whispered
the priest, throwing a troubled and searching glance
at the sick man. "For hours he reclines there, without speaking. Who could ever imagine that the
lively old man would be struck down so suddenly?"

"Ivan Stefanovitch," said one of the strangers in
a loud voice, and nearing the bed, "our right noble
Tzar, thy master, sends greeting. Bethink thyself!
Three Cossacks of thine that fled to him and told of

thy plotting against his authority, he gave orders to be taken prisoners ; and has sent them back to thee in gift. Ivan Stefanovitich, he but relies upon thy fidelity."

Inert and dull the eyes of Mazeppa disclosed themselves. His lips made motion. They but drove forth an incomprehensible murmur.

" We understand you," the Muscovites cried. " We understand you. You bless him, you thank him for his mercy ; and we are to inform him that eld has crushed your strength ; that every thought of yours is already turning on that which is not of this perishable earth."

" I fear," murmured the priest beside them, " that he is nearing the end."

The Tzar's messengers bowed their heads in sorrow, and retiring backwards went from the chamber.

Immediately they were without, the priest bolted the door.

" They are away," said he.

Instantly Mazeppa arose. He tore the plaster from his forehead, and threw it on the floor. His dark, wide-open eyes sparkled ; the colour came and went in his cheeks ; and under his fine curved nose his teeth showed themselves white and fresh like to those of a young man. He thrust the clothes aside, and sprang out of bed. From head to foot he was dressed, even to great coat and top-boots with spurs.

Gaily he poked the priest in the side.

" You little rogue of a priest ! Oh, ye vagabond ! In fair truth we've got ourselves out of the affair not badly, this time : in Moscow they will be believing, now, that old Mazeppa is lying on his back, all idle and out of mischief! God be good to them, simple souls! Ha, ha! You little blackguard of a priest! Oh, you hypocrite!"

The priest laughed drily. He was a deposed Bishop out of Bulgaria. His round head, with its short nose and far-receding eyes, resembled a dead man's skull.

Mazeppa became exceeding merry. "Mazeppa dying? Ask his little sweetheart. Just ask! Ho, you great Tzar of mine in Moscow, now we work to live and get rid of ye."

"The Tzar mistrusts you, my lord. But he will disarm you through his very magnanimity. 'Tis a way of his!"

"And, even so, he had overcome me if he had not dealt that blow on my ear the other night at table, when we were drunk. I hold my ear even as sacred as he does his ; and I never forgive an insult ; it rankles in my soul, and gnaws and gnaws at me. If I am no king by birth, I am of a kingly nature! And what can he do against my fine Cossacks? Eh! To business now. Narrate your adventure, you rogue!"

"My lord, clad as a beggar, I passed through the country to the Swedish Head-quarters : but on the way I fondled the change-house maids on my knee, and had my stoup of liquor by me at the table ; and if then I looked down and saw my toes peeping through the tattered leather, thought I about myself, Now, this is the Emissary of Mazeppa!"

" Good—good! How did you find, then, our buck ? "

" Buck ? "

" Of course! His Swedish Majesty! D'ye not think that he, beggarly appearance and all, must needs air himself even more than any perfumed Prince of France in silken stockings and all. And he has, too, that strange levity of the Northerner, who may knout one incessantly and shout : 'A mere trifle! It's just nothing! That won't hurt ye!' He has never been able to grieve over misfortune longer than the dark lasts ; that has been the secret of his strength. Alack for him and his fortune when once he lies, night after night, awake and brooding. I'm eager to see him. I long to meet him. But speak on."

" First, I found him in peruke and field dress on the aprons and kerchiefs of the tavern-girls ; then on the glasses out of which I drank ; on the sweet cakes I ate ; also on table-covers, box-lids, snuff-boxes ; and painted on the market stalls. Folk spoke of nothing save him ; and the children, placing themselves in line, played the game of God, his Swedish Servant. The people termed him the Protestant-Papist, Elect of God, reverently bowing thereat."

" Good! But how did you find him, himself, on reaching head-quarters ? "

" I warn you ; I foretell nothing good. I saw the worse tokens. I found him boastful and arrogant, like to some great man when the whole world bows down before him. Marlborough, after his audience in Saxony, left the camp shrugging his shoulders ; and

the sovereigns, too, began to laugh at him behind his
back ; his own generals become tired of him."

" Then you mean that he is become the common
folks' hero : even such a man I need, to gather
the wild hordes around me.   Unless you assure me
you have seen him eat and drink I'll not believe he's a
living man ! I would say, then, that the young Prince
of Sweden fell in the broil at Narva ; but his wraith
yet rides before the troops ; and the snow falls and
falls, and the benumbed battalions know not whither
he is leading them.   When the foe recognise him in
the cannon-smoke, all aghast they drop their muskets,
and durst not shoot ; and he knows not that oft-times
he cuts down men sinking on their knees in terror
before him. Hired bravos throw away their weapons
when his eye falls on them, and accuse themselves ;
he lets them go unpunished. Speak not to him of
kingdoms and dominions, and Settlements-in-Treaty.
Gold ?   Lands ?   From Austria he demanded a
chamberlain who had slandered him black as the very
Devil ; and a swarm of Russian soldiers fled thither ;
and liberty of conscience for the protestant folk.
From Prussia he got imprisonment of a Colonel who
had betrayed advices to the Tzar, and the banishment
of a writer who had criticised his remissions to the
bigots. From Saxony he demanded Patkull and all
deserters, and liberty for the Sobieskies and Saxons
gone over to Sweden.   He compelled King Augustus
to pack up in a velvet-lined box all the old Polish
regalia, and restore them to Stanislaus.   After he has
deposed King Augustus in Poland, he will cast down

the Tzar or challenge him to single combat. But as for their crowns and sovereignties, he will never have them in a present! Since the times of old no more strange individual has handled the sword or borne the sceptre."

Mazeppa, whilst speaking, had clung so vehemently to one of the bed-posts, that the plumes of the silken canopy nodded and nodded.

But the priest raised his third finger in the air.

"I have warned you," he answered. "All that comes in touch with him is doomed to death or destruction. In all truth he is a patron saint of adventure. He has invested adventure with eminence and endured it with steadfastness. And you too, my lord, are an adventurer! And myself am one of the most addicted. Therefore will I be submissive!"

He let his hand fall, and came nearer Mazeppa, with less respect in his air of familiarity.

"Ivan Stefanovitch, have you never conjectured why I directed my steps straight to your gates?"

"You got hunted off your Bishop's Stool through your unbeliefs and villainous pranks!"

"In main it was on account of a little trifling piece of pilfering. There were a couple of pearls in the iconastare?"

"Which ye, setting in their stead bits of glass, sold privily, to enable yourself to live somewhat easier and more worthy of a servant of the Church!"

"Let us talk no more of that! When I heard speak of Mazeppa, that famous page of Johannes Kasimir's Court, he that did pay homage to the seducing sex,

till in the end an over-jealous spouse had him bound
naked on the back of a horse and driven out into the
wilderness ; and there he founded his realm of adventure.   St. Andrew protect you, Mazeppa !   I needed
a Little Master, one too much ashamed to cut off a
good head, and who would suffer me to read in peace
my Greek and Machiavelli ; one to whom I could
say, 'Be it so, O master mine. All is but a phantasma.
Even this, that you are the over-lord and I am the
servant!'   Therefore came I to you.   But the blood
of the adventurer cannot now endure the restraint ;
and, of a truth, is got weary of thy watered wines,
for, Mazeppa, ye are a great miser !   So, seeing that
now you think to have a right affair with musket balls,
I follow you.   And since the Swedish King gives ear
no longer to his generals, nor to the beseeching letters
from his grandmother and his people, because that
the most dangerous and impracticable way of all tends
hither, he will accept your prayer to form an alliance.
With you and your Cossacks he will go against the
Tzar.   Here are the papers."

The priest, throwing aside his cloak, stood in Cossack dress, with pistols in his belt.   He withdrew one
much-folded document from his breast.   Mazeppa
grew pale, and seized it, and held it long pressed
against his mouth, whilst inclining his forehead and
bowing himself as if before some invisible holy
picture.

" The drums—the drums," he stammered in excitement.   But when the priest was even at the door, he
called him back.   "No! let the drums be beat at the

first of the morning." Then he stepped to a simple
wooden table in the ante-chamber and seated himself
at his accounts.

His stewards he called together, and cast the
reckonings for, and bade them observe greater fru-
gality. A raider, yet a wise and economical owner,
he himself in the end overlooked the packing of his
many coffers and chests, and occasionally also helped.
The next morning he clad himself in an old, rich
embroidered Cossack hablement. All in a flurry, he
no sooner sat down than he sprang up again. He
remained standing before the mirror for nigh an hour,
and stroking now and then again his moustaches
with his small, delicate white hands. As soon as the
drums were rolled he sprang into the saddle, and incessantly kept his horse at the gallop.

One morning, some time after, he was riding
in the King's retinue through the snowstorm. The
priest urged his horse, as if by chance, alongside him.
All around, the troops were marching, soiled with dirt,
their weapons and cannon shielded against corrosion ;
baggage wagons rattled onward, creaking under loads
of commissariat, the sick, and covered coffins.

Drunk Zaparogs, prancing Cossacks, and vigorously trumpeting Poles rode about, clad in their
green and red cloaks, and with tall, tinkling, brass
helmets ; some flourished lances decked with tassels
and tags, or long muskets inlaid with silver and
ivory ; others, again, played strange and mournful
tunes on wooden flutes. It was somewhat of a
romantic march, through unbeaten and unknown

forest tracts, across frozen swamps, and beneath snow-laden firs, into the enigmatical East.

"Mazeppa," began the priest in a low voice, "ye promised to join the Swedes with 30,000 Cossacks, but only 4000 followed thee!"

Mazeppa let his sorrel unchecked leap into a gallop, and nodded in silence. But the priest was grown tired of being fooled.

"The day before yesterday the half of your following took fright. Yesterday, yet more. Soon but 200 will remain, only the dwarfs that guard your coffers and two tons of ducats. Your fellow conspirators are seized; your towns are burnt; your few trusty servants bound to planks and cast headlong into the river. Soon ye will be naught but a spruce cavalier in the following of the Swedish King!" On Mazeppa saying naught, the priest continued; "This day I also abandon ye: the Swedish small beer is too sour, to my taste! and my toes gape over-much in my footgear. Thy Emissary, O Mazeppa, requires a richer master! Farewell, Ivan Stefanovitich"

Mazeppa answered: "So long as I still have my head on my shoulders and retain my philosophy, I remain Mazeppa. Whilst my Cossacks turn and flee, I bid the staff and insignia of hetman be borne before me; and ride on again to the King, as if the millions of Xerxes were behind me. And he, for all his impoverished kingdom, his malcontent generals, and his waning fame, receives me like to the most felicitated of Princes. What matters it to him or myself how many ride behind us? He has a sufficiency of kingly

honours : will be the most favoured of God.   He looks
on this venture as a love-sick swain on his beloved.
Through his birthright he will not win favour, but
from himself !   And should we two, he and I, be the
last of living men, and hid in a burrow in the steppe,
despite all will we maintain our diversion in philosophy,
and mutually pay honour to each other an we were
sitting before a Coronation Banquet."

" You speak of his setting sun.   You have read the
signs aright !   He cannot open his mouth without
boasting like a very baggage knave."

" Easy it is for one to have modesty when others sing
his praises ! " And with a proud gesture Mazeppa flung
back his curled white locks, then galloped to the King,
who saluted him, bending again and again in his saddle.

In their vicinity some of the generals busied themselves in talking loud, so that the King could hear
them.

Said Anders Lagerkrona : " When I get to Moscow,
I'll patch the seat of my riding breeches with the
Tzar's nightcap ! "

" Shame on you ! " rejoined Axel Sparre.   " D'ye
not know an old saying, that in time to come, a Sparre
is to be Governor at the Kremlin ? "

" Hear ! " cried the ensigns.   " Shoot him down,
that durst hinder so great and illustrious a Prince
from accomplishing his end ! "

The King laughed and hummed : " The Russian is
to run ! The Russian is to run ! " But when the
speakers were beyond his ear, their faces changed, and
their demeanours became vehement and melancholic.

"Your Majesty!" cried Mazeppa, in sorry Latin, with gleaming eyes, "So far might your all-conquering arms be thrust forward now that of a fine morning we be scarce eight miles from Asia!"

"On that must the learned dispute," answered the King, all amused, but seeking for the Latin words, and gazing on Mazeppa's white, comely hands. "If the boundary be not so far off, we must find it; and thus be able to say that we, too, have been in Asia!"

And in time their voices died away.

The priest reined in his horse.

"Asia!" he murmured. "Asia lays not in the middle of Europe, my lords! Ride on, ride on, my right venturesome masters. I have so often changed my garb and name, that none of your Swedes have made out to a certainty who I am. But do you forget not, it was the beggarly monk, that vagabond, Mazeppa's emissary, who, through cunning parleying, laid his finger, blue with frost, down on thy fate, and on that of thy Demi-God, when in the steppes he discovered to you the way. Thou art right, King Karolus! And thou, also, Mazeppa! All, all in the end, rests on one isolated individual."

It snowed and snowed; but still he sat motionless on his thin nag while the battalions drew by, silent and long-suffering. The last of the soldiers, turning round, looked at the solitary horseman, unknown to them, and stared at his small, death-like features; then, taken with sinister affright, hurried onward.

CHAPTER IX.

FIFTEEN YEARS LATER.

WHEN the porridge was eaten, and the two tallow candles by the pewter dish were half burnt, seats were drawn in towards the fire. The residence was one of the smallest and poorest in the neighbourhood, but this night one marked a lack of nothing. On the floor the straw lay like a soft carpet; fresh twigs of juniper were stuck sideways in the obscured, rain-bespattered window panes; the radiance of the fire on the open hearth streamed yellow on the whitewashed wooden walls; and over and above, a stoup of liquor had gone the round just a short time past. Everyone knew that now was come the hour of jollity. The two serving-maids, who had donned their best, worsted bodices, cleared the board as tardily as possible, and remained standing by the door, for Höök, the old Captain, the Karolinean, tobacco-box in hand, had taken the seat of honour before the fire. But first he made himself feel right comfortable, after he had drawn off his heavy boots, sewn with cobblers' thread, and set his feet in their thick white stockings, one upon the other at the edge of the hearth, to get them thoroughly warmed.

In truth, that night he had already taken all the talk to himself, relating even about Ehrenkrona, who had received the Sword of Honour from Frederick, the Danish King, but had made no more over it other than taking it along with him in a box. This time, however, the Captain assumed an earnest and settled demeanour, and went on to a fresh tale. In the main it was considered that he lied most inveterate; but none concerned themselves: all the importance was, that he told a good story.

He was an oldish man, with a snub nose bitten blue with frost; his smooth hair and moustache, curled like to a youth's, had aye been so fair, that no one noticed if the years had whitened them here and there. Moreover, in his short, tight-buttoned tunic, he sat sturdy and straight as ever.

"Yes," he began, in his wonted method, "that autumn I lost myself in the forest, things went ill with me. I mean that time in Severia. Lewenhaupt had destroyed our baggage, and was taking us along the Soza river, to find a safe place for fording; his purpose being, that later on we were to join the King on the other side. Now many of the foot stayed behind to plunder the baggage. I was an ensign at that time, and was sent back, with a few others, by General Mayor Stachelberg, to bring these men to reason; but already the Muscovite was at them; and I hardly yet know how in the darkness it came that I saved myself by swimming across the river.

"Dripping with water and mud, I happened on a dragoon at the far side. He was of my own regiment,

and we called him Long Jan, because he was one of
the tallest and the thinnest that ever bore a Swedish
weapon. His chest was spare, but his hands were
large. His arms and legs seemed to have not a sinew
in them ; and his lean and simple face, recognisable
by any from its slanting mouth and thick nether-lip,
was wholly bare—not a hair grew on it. God knows
why he was ever taken along with us!

"At this time, however, I was as glad to see his
meagre person as ever my sweetheart ; and as fast as
our legs could take us we made off at random, to warm
ourselves and dry our clothes ; then towards break of
day we threw ourselves down and slept. For many
days we held on in this fashion, through forests and
marshes, and all the time our clothes were never right
dry. Once we took them off, and hung them on a
bough ; yet that helped but little in the damp autumn
air ; and they were none the better ; only much colder
when we put them on again with much trouble. And
our boots ! It was just impossible to take them off.
Betimes they got dried in the walking, but soon got as
wet as ever in a morass ; and one burst of rain
followed on another. I had a small piece of bacon and
some black bread, which I shared with my taciturn
and as it appeared submissive comrade in misfortune ;
and after this was finished, we chewed leaves and bark
and everything eatable we happed on. Our hunger did
not cause such a death-like pain as did the constant
fatigue. And by degrees all strength began to go,
and our limbs became so stiff, that we could not rest
without torture.

" But one night we heard, of a sudden, the barking of a dog. For some minutes I felt as if I burned alive with joy, but immediately sense came back, and I thought on the danger. So I turned in the opposite direction, and Long Jan followed, silent as ever. When we had walked for some time, I noted that we only came nearer to the sound. I took the soldier by the arm, and set myself in another direction ; yet, as if forced by some hidden irresistible temptation, despite every effort, we came aye the nearer to the sound.

" When in the end I let go Jan's arm, he stepped out faster than afore.

" ' Halt ! ' I cried after him. For, though I was terribly suffering from fatigue, I had no wish to walk straight into an enemy's house, where in all probability the very best axe was awaiting us.

" ' Halt, halt ! ' Jan repeated obediently, but for all that he ran on again.

" I rushed after him and brought him to a stand. So long as I had a grip, he kept steady and motionless. As soon as I let go, he began to run once more.

" ' Halt ! Stand still,' I thundered, all enraged as if under fire. I was fairly confounded at this sudden mutinous waywardness of a man trained in our iron discipline. ' Will ye not obey your own ensign, fellow ? '

" ' Halt ! Stand still,' he repeated, but continued to gallop as before, just as if he was no more the master of his own feet.

" ' In Jesu's name, then,' cried I, ' things cannot be worse than they are ! But then, ye've now turned yourself into an ensign, for ye are of the ranks ; and me into the private? Well and good then! But forget it not!'

"Long Jan did not answer. Maybe he did not even hear me. So then I had to follow him.

"After some minutes we reached an open plain, with secluded houses and barns on it. Before us stood a great wooden building of several stories. The rain-drops on the moss, which made watertight the walls consisting of huge tree trunks, glistened in the rays of the drooping sun; and the window panes gleamed as if lit with countless candles; but the door was shut, and no smoke came out of the chimneys. The place was like to a stricken body, with closed mouth and lack-ing breath, but with eyes, that all sinister, were illumed with baneful light from without. Behind a haystack, slanting and tumbled down, cringed a dog tied to a stake. On seeing us it wagged its tail.

"Jan stepped straight up to the door, and knocked, but no one opened.

"Thereupon he drew his sword, and with the handle beat in the nearest window. Instantly we heard a frightened woman's voice crying 'Varvara!' many times.

"The shattered glass jingled to the floor. The lead casing of the window was all bent and broken. We heard hasty footsteps in the house. Almost that moment the door was opened by a slender and stately serving maid; a broad plait of bright hair hanging down her back; and on her little black cap, as on her tight-fitting red and green bodice, numberless silver coins were dangling. In her hand she held an unlit lanthorn, presumably picked up through force of habit in her terror.

" ' We will do no harm,' said I, trying to speak correctly in that difficult tongue. ' The Lord keep us from such horrors, Mademoiselle. . . . But we are starving, and before everything we must——'

" ' Have dry clothing,' interrupted Long Jan, his teeth all chittering.

" It was the first time during our long wanderings that I had heard this strange fellow speak of his own free will. And now into the bargain he had the effrontery to take the words out of my very mouth!

" When the girl, turning round, left the door half-open, he stepped to the side, however, to give me place.

" Said I, to him in irritation, ' The Ensign must aye go first ! '

" ' God keep me from that ! ' he answered, his spurs clashing together in salute.

" But half glad at our peaceful reception, and yet half angry, I continued to say, with some sharpness in my tones, that he could not doubt my earnestness : ' Or the Devil take the Ensign, then ! '

" At that he drew his long body through the half-open door.

" We found ourselves in a great hall, the house having no vestibule. In the middle of it the stove, built of many coloured Dutch tiles, rose like a tower. Along the walls, that were made of the rough-hewn tree trunks, thickly packed with moss, stood some black envarnished seats, and on a dresser glittered pewter utensils.

K

" The serving maid ran hither and thither, crying on Varvara, who at last appeared, heavy with sleep and all in terror, in the furthest corner of the dark place. There the two of them stood trembling and whispering in alarm. After a little they grew calmer, and on my addressing them to their surprise as ' Mademoiselles,' and acting as if I did not know them to be but poor bond-maids, they could not but exchange glances and appear more amiable. It was all like a drop of hot oil on the creaking wagon.

" They told us, now that their folk had gone away, some two weeks past, at the first whisper of the Swedish invasion. Moreover they assured us that nothing of any worth was left in the house, and that they would willingly do their best to be of avail to us.

" Varvara had beautiful teeth and black curly hair, but was too small, too thick. She likewise laughed in a loud and ringing manner, that affected me unpleasantly. The golden-locked maid, called Katharina, I could well endure ; and could not but pinch her ear as she was carrying in the wood for the stove.

" Meantime, Jan, without more delay, had taken off his tattered blue tunic, and as he owned neither vest nor shirt, he soon stood naked to the skin, in all his pitiful thinness. So that no one there but himself could keep from merriment. Never at any time had I seen a flicker of amusement on his stiff countenance.

" After each of us had got a sheep's skin, and satisfied our hunger for the most, we laid ourselves on the

stove, our swords between our knees. I also ventured
to bid the ensign keep alternate watch with me, lest
they assail us unawares. I also forbade the two
women to leave the hall, and then, aloud in Swedish,
I commended us to the protection of the Almighty.
But oft-times He has it that we men occasion our
own surprises!

"As no one spoke to me, I slept peaceful and long,
till I became awakened by stinging heat; I had better
have said a torture. But at any rate it made me recollect
that I was no more a wandering skeleton, but a living
man. And now imagine my panic when I saw the
suffocating place was dark and untenanted, but heard
shrieks and cries from out the neighbouring room.
Instantly I seized my sword, and leaping to the door,
thrust it open. Then I perceived a raging kitchen
fire, and before it Jan, clothed in a chequered dressing-
gown of bright cashmere, and with high-heeled shoes.

"Apparently the rascal had some talent for foraging:
a fowl was already on the spit; and into a boiling
kettle he was throwing every eatable he could lay
hands on. Between times he took one rare goblet
after another out of a rifled cupboard before him,
smashed them against the edge of the hearth, and
threw the fragments on the floor.

"I leapt forward, and clasped the rapscallion round
the body; but was not in a state to make him budge.
His untoward obstinacy lent the strength of a giant
to his weakened body; I myself was yet exhausted
with past sufferings. On him turning his face to me,
I noted that his eyes were glassy and fixed, and a

K—2

strong smell of liquor came from him.   I let him
stumble free, all stupified.   He was drunk!

" Golden-haired Katharina, as much amused as
troubled, meantime came to me and told me in her
soft voice.   . . .   Humph! At that time Höök, the
old Captain, was a young and comely fellow . . . !

" Where were we then ?   Yes, she told me that Jan
had gone from room to room, and broken everything,
vases as well as clocks.   In the end he had gone
through every section of the cellar below, except one,
the key to which was lost.   She added hastily : ' But,
then, you, poor man, will likewise be very hungry ; '
and shoved me into another room of the most rare
splendour.

" On its walls hung green tapestry enwrought with
Diana Hunting.   The most priceless vestments lay
about on the shiny floor : the leathern chairs were all
gilt ; and beside a dish in the middle of the table, stood
jars filled with clear, golden wine; not kvass or beer.

" Now at the sight of so much splendour I lost my
senses, and my distrust became somewhat dashed,
for both serving-maids appeared totally content in
being able for once to dissipate and destroy things,
and likewise felt themselves on unfriendly ground
in the very house where formerly they served as
bond women, all humble and submissive. To them,
'twas plainly an intoxication of victory, to be able
to waste the dainties which hitherto they had never
durst touch ; to throw themselves into fine carved
chairs, before which they had had to curtsey low ; to
trample under foot valuable clothes, which aforetime

they had not been thought even worthy enough to touch.

" They chose for me a coat of stiff silver brocade, its skirts stiffened with whalebone, so that they looked as baggy as women's ; and on my feet, from which the previous night I had cut off the boots with great difficulty, they put silk stockings and scarlet shoes. All the same I never ventured to lay aside my sword, for I could not away with the notion of some subtle treachery.

" With full simple frankness of a very Queen of hearts, Katharina clapped her hands, soft as they were white, and confessed that she was really amused, for with me, who was on the same footing, they could be and do as they wished ; but concerning the Ensign, maybe a great Lord, they had to be on their guard.

" I seated myself at table on one of the leathern chairs, my glistering coat tails almost concealing it. On each side of me I bade one of the maids take her place ; and I clinked glasses with them, and drank right heavily.

" ' The ensign is of very noble parts,' said I. ' Perhaps he may become a Councillor ! ' At that time my worst curse was on people that fought with the pen.

" ' But Mademoiselles will know full well, that the nobility sometime through an unlucky dispensation, be born as simple-witted as wayward : that is the reason, then, why I sometimes think myself obliged, so to speak, to lead his understanding aright ! '

" As a soldier, I have had aye one fault.   'Tis true,

I have dealt blows at the right time, and could safeguard myself; but in the main, I have been docile
and somewhat too soft hearted. So now I let Jan
run riot in the kitchen, as it pleased him; and myself
ate and drank to my heart's content. But with every
gulp, I felt how the liquor was robbing me of my
senses. And the reason that I became not im-
portunate with my merry hostesses, was less owing
to virtue, with which the Almighty often invests, and
prudently, too, the beauty in a woman, than to my
fatigue, which was now affecting me like a sleeping
potion. Caution advised me to set aside the bumper;
but after the hardships of the last few days, the wine
was irresistible.

"I sank into sleep, sitting there, my hands crossed
over my sword hilt. 'Now I hear lurking footsteps,'
said I to myself, in dreams, 'They are aye coming
near me, here, behind my chair! I must draw my
sword in haste. But what is it?—I can stir neither
hand nor foot, for all I'm so awake that I can make
out Diana and her hounds on the hanging. All the
air is but a swirling mist playing round the faces of
the chattering girls, and the flames of the tapers. I
am clean drunk! There's no doubt on't! But now
I'll go asleep again. Again, there are the lurking
footsteps behind my chair. A serf stands there, with
his axe. This very moment he's raising it. The
next, I'll be feeling it like a stroke of lightning on my
neck . . . and then all is over! Why may the
chair not keep still? I can't keep myself steady if
you leap. B-r-r, horse! Do you know aught on this

earth that's able to frighten me! But to keep myself turned on the haunches of a galloping steed of the King. . . . I cannot! Yes, you see well enough, I'm lying here in all the mud of the street. Fah! Why are you laughing? And the vault in the cellar. . . . Why did ye just say that one . . . one . . . one, two, one two, one two, boys blue, two, three, with powder and lead, three, four, we're serving, four, five, land and country, five, six, Carolus Rex. . . ."

" Twas then I raised myself up on my elbows, and sang the whole of the Sixth Psalm, from the first to the very last verse, and this, with so stout a voice, that all evil needs in terror betake itself. Many a time I have had a drunken rally, but never one that gave me more agony!

" Awakening betimes next morning, I sprang up from the floor where I had been lying on my back under the chair. Certain was I, now, of falling into some ambuscade; and, therefore, was overjoyed to find both the maids asleep on a sheep-skin by the table. But without, in the kitchen, I heard strange noises. There I found an old one-eyed hag, Natalia by name, and a hairy serf, called Makar, especially resembling him of my dream. They confessed that they had kept themselves close, but had crept out on noting that we intended no evil. They also related that many inhabitants of the town near by, on learning of our arrival, had put their goods and chattels on wagons during the night, and gone off at full gallop.

" I felt myself now free of suspicion, and in my joy

went back into the room, and bending over charming
Katharina, still slumbering, warmly kissed her. She
awoke somewhat, laughed softly, and turned on her
other side to go asleep again. But I kissed her anew.
This time she defended herself; and then sprang up,
wide awake and amused.

" 'You're a charming girl, Katharina; and I mistrust you no longer,' said I. ' Get me now fresh
water and something salt.'

" Whilst she came and went, serving the breakfast,
I often slipped my arm round her waist—not too slender
was it—and kissed her. In the end, she kissed me,
and, pressing close on me, sometimes grew merry,
sometimes sad.

" To and fro we went through the many chambers.
But when before a certain door she aye was very discreet in her behaviour, for in the room beyond it my
lord the ensign was pleased to rest himself in one of
the most princely beplumed beds.   In the end we
seated ourselves in a great chair of fine yellow leather,
and I took her on my knee, and caressed her thick
tresses.   It was no untruth I told when I murmured
in her ear that the hardened heart of a soldier had
seldom beat faster.   I lose myself in melancholy when
thinking of the happy times that followed ; and rather
than recall them hour for hour, I leave it to you folk, in
particular to the younger, to image them all; and
right lively ones, too !

"Every night, nevertheless, I ordered Makar to
keep watch before the house, and never laid aside my
sword. Frequently Katharina was wont to snatch it

from my side, then carry it before her, both hands round the hilt. Up and down the room she would parade with it, while the autumn rains crackled on the panes, and I had good cheer. The loose hangings would wave behind her in her careering, the pictures taking on life. The walls re-echoed her when, with her little black cap drawn down over her head like a warrior, she cried, ' Forward—Charge.' Then I built barricades of tables and gilt leather chairs ; till in the end I leapt forward into the very midst of the attack, and secured the weapon-bearer as well as the weapon. Never a thought took I of my comrades, who mayhap were starving and bleeding for our King. My one desire was aye to remain there.

" Katharina was aye smelling of lavender. We kept for ourselves a nook, close under lock and key ; and in here she had lugged her great chest, which was covered over and over with blue chequered paper. It contained her clothes and other belongings, and was never opened but the odour of lavender filled the whole chamber. Her greatest delight was to go down on her knees, and take out all her clothes and a great number of boxes ; and pack them in again with even greater care than afore. When all this seemed too tedious to me, or the room now and then got too cold, I persuaded her to go into the hall with me and seat ourselves on the stove.

" Then I tried to take her attention with tales of the adventures of my broad-sword, and on occasion was not sparing with my words. I knew of a certainty it had already taken eleven men's lives, and could show on my arm marks of gunshot wounds and sword-cuts. But she did not ask much about all this!

"Then, when I told her the tales of Prince Gideon of Maxibrandar, she grew peevish.

"'For all that, such a thing never happened!' quoth she, beginning with vigour to sow red and green scalloping on a pair of lacing boots. One plainly saw that they needs became a masterpiece in their kind.

"My Lord the Ensign lived in continual drunkenness, and showed a high disdain of both women. Katharina maintained she found this very agreeable, seeing that it was awkward for a woman of her class to reprove an aristocrat if he importuned. However, one morning the ensign bethought himself of the close vault below, which both of us had forgotten.

"Down went he. Straightway Katharina got so carried away with terror, that she could not suppress tokens of it. Squeezing both my hands, she implored me to keep him back. So completely was I the captive of my heart, that although my former mistrust was now revived, I found myself ready to help her.

"We went after him, and found him already busy breaking open the locked door, which was of wood.

"'Leave it alone!' I ordered.

"He answered, 'Yes!' but with imperturbable obstinacy continued to crash on the door.

"Thereupon I excused myself to my sobbing companion by saying that a mere private like myself could not command his officer. The next moment the wood gave way. Within the vault a lamp was burning under a gilded Russian picture of the Virgin, and alongside a bed stood a table covered with various victuals. Between the bed and the wall moved something dark and roundish, which, when we neared, was recognised to be the shoulders of an old man.

"When he saw he was discovered, he crept out, and embracing the knees of the ensign implored for mercy. He avowed himself to be the master of the house, and that he had hidden himself here after having sent away his family ; also he promised to be our trusty servant if we would but spare his life.

"' Be calm,' I answered, helping the trembling ancient from the ground. ' Now ye'll be our drummer, when we sit at meat ! '

"That night we sat down to a sumptuous meal. My lord the ensign, as was his wont, occupied the chief seat, and myself and Katharina sat beside him.

"On a table a little to the left of us stood the white-haired, shaking old noble, with a brass mortar and pestle in his hand, and Makar with two pot-lids. They thwacked their kitchen utensils in time with the beat of the melancholy folk-song sung by ugly old Natalia sitting between them on the table.

"I know not the reason, but her wailing voice bereft me of my lively spirits, and I began thinking on the many many thousands of my far-away fellows. Between my vest and shirt I carried a big packet of letters from anxious relatives to near and dear ones in the field ; and these they had prayed on me to deliver when I reached the King's encampment.

" I withdrew them from my breast ; they held no secrets from me ; for on my last night in Riga I had received many of them unsealed.   Drawing a candle nearer me, I glanced at random through one of them. It was writ in a shaky hand.   Thus it read : ' Give this into the hand of Hans.   My dear son, receive the blessing of thý father, though parted far from him by land and sea, and soon near to that world where crocodiles, scorpions, and other creeping things strike fear into man.   .   .   .'

" I felt the sacred responsibility of the delivery of this benediction.   My conscience grew heavier and heavier.   Maybe my face showed my feelings.   I noted that Katharina pressed my foot more than usual. But I did but press it in return, and deemed it to be only a love token.

" On re-folding the note, I saw that nevertheless she sat there pale as a corpse, and touching neither meat nor sup.   So that she might whisper to me, I bent somewhat in to her.   But the old noble on the table stared fixedly at her, whilst more zealously than ever he beat his uplifted mortar like a bell.

" I grew perplexed, and knew not what to employ for a pretext.   Then I bethought myself on saying that I was cold.   I got up, and went into the sleeping chamber ; and searching around in the darkness, cried : ' Katharina, my lass, where have ye put my sheepskin ? '

" When she came in, she threw herself on my neck.

" ' Heard ye not ? " she whispered, ' Makar telling

the master in all that noise, that he has got more than
sixty serfs together ? As soon as he gives them the
signal, by breaking the window in the hall, they'll
burst in and cut ye both down.'

" I remained somewhat steady, and sought to comfort her ; but, with her voice thick with tears, she told
further that at the outset she might have taken a part
in ensnaring us, yet that now she did not believe she
could live a day without me. Pressing her closer, I
kissed her burning mouth and beating forehead. But,
despite everything, at that very moment I experienced
a strange peace in my soul, for, of a sudden, our
acquaintanceship was soon to be a thing of the past.
Later on I have bitterly repented me, aye and
wondered at myself, that I had so little to give her in
all sweet faith, that parting hour. But I know naught
else to blame, except the reading of the letter and the
instant danger.

" ' If I could take you with me,' I stammered in a
low voice.

" I could plainly discern her in the half-light from
the opened door. She shook her head, and drew me
to the window, and besought me to get out and away.
Thereupon I burst into anger as it had been, and
shoved her far over the polished floor.

" Cried I, in a loud voice. ' What do ye take me
for, girl ? ' And with that I drew my sword, and
went back into the hall.

" When the ensign saw me thus, he leapt from the
table, and in a flash also drew his blade.

" Thereupon the old man raised his pestle to throw

it at the window. Instantly we stood before him, threatening him with our swords.

" In his mortal fear his knees knocked together.

" He cowered more and more, the pestle almost falling out of his hand. Natalia, holding her peace, crossed herself; and Makar, seeing his master was on the point of swooning, let his pot-lids clatter on the floor, and took him from behind, under the shoulders.

" He tried to wrest the pestle away for himself, yet the ancient only held it firmer. For a good time then we stood there, fronting each other, and without in the kitchen we heard the kettle singing. But soon we also heard clattering footsteps, for the serfs, spying through the window, had witnessed the affair. The doorway soon became packed tight with dirty sheepskins, and among them a bald forehead showing here and there. Then a shot cracked, and the smoke spread out over the matted heads. ·

" I forgot about our play at ensign and private, and made to shove Jan aside, to essay against them; but now I was to find out in all truth whom I had for a comrade. Jan stood as stiff as ever. Budge he would not. He even took me by the arms and thrust me aside with irresistible power.

" ' Ensign, ye've made me into the ensign and yourself into the private. Ye'll know our custom ?—that an officer leads.' And like a clap of thunder he burst among the sheepskins, his big broad hands clasped firm about the sword hilt. Now over his head the blade crashed into the wood of the door, now ripped up both clothes and flesh,

" I heard another report, and saw axes and pitch-forks all around. Jan let fall his arm that was be-ginning to gout with blood, and now could only wield his weapon with one hand ; but I was at his side, hacking and stabbing at them. We were pressed into a corner of the kitchen ; and my out-spreading coat-tails got torn into rags, the black whale-bone sticking out in all directions.

" Blackened with smoke till he was nigh irrecognis-able, Jan tottered, and fell against my shoulder. Seiz-ing his unwounded hand I pressed it like a brother's.

" Cried I to him. ' Now I know who ye are, Jan, and once we're out of this with whole skins we'll aye betogether.'

" He did not reply. One of his eyes was closed up ; the other, wide open. With a heavy thud he stotted on the floor. And this was the last I saw of Long Jan, the man at whom I had so often laughed, and who had angered me so frequently, but to whom I had shown through the grip of my hand that I esteemed him friend and equal.

" At first I tried to take care of his body, but speedily saw the uselessness of this last office. So a minute later I was once more amid the bushwood, but with a wound on my forefinger.

" I had the luck, however, to fall in with some twenty other Swedes, also strayed. Up a fir tree I climbed then, to make out the occasion of a long streak of fiery reflection in the murky heavens overhead.

" ' What see ye ? ' asked my fellows.

" ' I see pitch darkness. But on shutting my eyes

I see more.   Then I see an enemy's camp before me ;
below me, marshy ground that almost sucks up our feet
in its desire to be the deathbed of a few poor, wretched
soldiers ; behind me I mark unbounded waste land,
where the bodies of our brothers lie livid and rotting
under the October leaves, where no fowl cackles before
the burnt courtyards, and the horses find no fodder but
of tree bark.   Farther behind lays the sea ; and behind
the waters I see a long road, its signposts all decayed,
that leads up to a red, poverty-stricken house.   Inside
it the starving fare has just been removed from table,
and while the venerable old man takes out the book
in which a goose feather lays as a marker at the First
of Revelations, he sinks into thought, wondering if
now we at last have joined the King with the rein-
forcements, and if now his dear ones, maybe this very
hour, try to make out his scarce readable letter.'

" 'Tis true I did not say all this at the time, but I
know, I thought the like, for by now Katharina was
almost gone from my mind.

" ' What see ye now ? ' asked my comrades.   ' Ye've
climbed higher ! '

" Far away over the trees I saw beacons or camp fires
as they had been lumps of molten iron in the murky
night vapour ; the series of peaked tents there recalled
some foggy coast showing out in a beacon flare.

" ' This fine light,' said I in a low voice to them,
' is like to a goodly apple into which over many pips
are stuck ; and we must have our swords ready.   But,
hush !   Wait . . .   that was not Russian !   Hear
ye the outposts calling to each other ?   As true as I

live was that not our own dear mother-tongue? If I have not heard "To the Devil" at least seven times, the Devil take me!'

"I don't remember how I came down out of that tree. But on all sides I was shaking outstretched hands, and fell out of one embrace into another among the yellow-and-blue coats. Ay, how many longed-for greetings had I to deliver at this desolate end of the earth! How many adventures to relate!

"Half-carried, half-shoved, I went further into the camp; and was almost brought to a stand with their peals of laughter, when they marked my tattered foppery, with its whalebones flapping about at every movement. But, for myself, I verily shouted in joy.

"'I have a letter for Captain Bagge,' cried I.

"'Killed, long ago.'

"'Also one for Cederstjerna, a Lieutenant.'

"'Killed ——.'

"I stumbled over a dead horse lying agrin in my way, and almost burnt by the glowing logs of a neighbouring fire. The rain had put out the flames, but in the illumed space behind it I saw some sinister-looking officers seated in a circle. On the ground before them a man was outstretched; his fur cap drawn well over his forehead, and the collar of his cloak pulled high up.

"I waved the packet of letters, and made to step over him. A hand clutched me by the shoulder. Quick and sternly was I checked by the words:

"'Are ye mad? See ye not, it is his Majesty?'

"Then in salute I brought my heels together, and

L

raised my hand with the letters to my head, and tears starting to my eyes fell down my cheeks. . ."

Captain Höök got up after ending his tale, and bade goodnight.   But when he was out, and in the entry, the others heard him stop stockstill on the stairs.

So one of the serving maids drew on her worsted jacket, loosened the last candle end from the plate, and with her hand beneath it, to prevent any of the burning wick falling among the straw, she went out to light the captain over the way.   All knew that he never liked to cross by himself, because in the pit of the night, he, the Karolinean, became afraid.

CHAPTER X.

THE BELEAGUERED HOUSE.

SURPRISED by the biting cold of winter, the Swedes had taken up their quarters behind the ramparts of Hadjatsk, thronging in with great confusion. Soon not a house was to be found which was not crowded with frost-bitten and dying soldiery. Their agonised cries were echoing into the streets, and their amputated fingers, feet, and limbs, lay thrown out on the stone steps. The wagons had come in fast, one after the other; and were now all at a stand from the town gates to the market place; and so close packed, that the frost-bitten troopers streaming by had to creep between the wheels and the sledge runners.

The horses, sorely lacerated by chafing harness and white with rime, were cowering away from the snarling wind. They had got no fodder for many days, nor had anyone attended to them. Some of their drivers sat frozen to the box-seats, their hands still stuck into the cuffs of their great coats.

Some of the conveyances were like huge boxes or coffins. Through the chinks in their flat tops one marked faces sad and sullen, some bent over prayer-books, some enfevered and full of yearning, staring at

L—2

the sheltering houses by them. Thousands of poor wretches, in undertones or in the recesses of their hearts, besought the Lord for mercy.

The soldiery stood in long lines by the ramparts; many of them had red Cossack cloaks buttoned over their tattered uniforms, and sheepskins about their naked feet. Wood pigeons and sparrows, frozen so stark, that one could catch them with the hand, had perched themselves on the heads and shoulders of the dead still standing erect there; and pitifully they flapped their wings on the chaplains coming forward to administer to the dying the last Sacrament. It was served with brandy.

In the market place, between two burnt-out sites stood a great house, out of which loud voices were resounding. A soldier delivered a bundle of faggots to a cornet standing in the doorway. On regaining the street he shrugged his shoulders.

Said he to a fellow of his, hearing the noise : " It's only the officers of the Chancellery quarrelling ! "

The cornet at the door was newly arrived in the Lewenhaupt command. He took the faggots into the room, and threw them on the hearth; instantly the officers became silent. But as soon as he had closed the door behind him, their voices burst out louder than before.

It was his Excellency, Count Piper, himself, with frowning face, cheeks all aglow, and quivering nostrils, who was standing in the middle of the chamber.

" And I think the whole affair is naught but folly," he cried. " Folly ! Folly ! "

Hermelin, of the pointed nose, kept his eyes and hands in motion, and sprang about like to a small tame rat. But beside the hearth, Field Marshal Rehnskiöld, handsome and of a fine carriage, was murmuring unintelligible words, and humming softly to himself. Had he not muttered and hummed, the trouble had now been to seek, all present being in fair accord for once ; but his continual muttering and twittering to himself, instead of either speaking out or keeping silent, was not to be endured.

Lewenhaupt, standing by the window, took snuff and clappered the lid of his box. His brown eyes were near out of his head ; and his odd peruke, as it were, was growing bigger and bigger. If Rehnskiöld had not been there with his aggravating mouthing, Lewenhaupt had controlled himself as ever. But at present his anger over-mastered him.

He clacked to the lid of his snuff-box for the last time. Between his teeth broke out the loud murmur : " I am not anxious that his Majesty should busy himself in state-craft. But of late he also thinks of leading the troops ! Has he ever shown right judgment at any reconnoitre or attack ? Trained and tried veterans, who never can be replaced, he throws away day after day in futile and useless actions of bravado. If our men storm a rampart he thinks there is no need of them to use fascines, and so they get mercilessly massacred. In plain truth, my sirs, I can excuse a studiosus Upsaliensis many stupid deeds, but I think otherwise of a general in castris. Surely it is for the good of none to go into action under such a leader ! "

"And so," replied Piper, "his Majesty does not trouble my Lord the General, just now, with too important a command! At first, before anyone succeeded in winning the preference, all went better; but now his Majesty must aye be playing the mediator between ye all! The continual smirking he needs employ drives a man mad!"

He gesticulated with his arms. He had talked himself into a fury, lost to sense and control, for all he was at one with Lewenhaupt.

Even as he spoke, he turned about and left the room. The door fell to with such a crash that Rehnskiöld saw fit to redouble his whistling and muttering. Had he only yet said something. But no, he would not!

Gyllenkrook, sitting at the table and busily revising the march route, was red with anger.

Said a small, withered General, whispering maliciously into his ear: "Diamond earrings for Piper's Countess, maybe, might help Lewenhaupt into another post!"

Had Rehnskiöld now made an end to all his fooling then perhaps Lewenhaupt had been able to master himself; and taking out the reports which he carried beneath his great coat, had taken a seat by the table. But, instead, he was now incensed even more; and he, too, wont to be taciturn and orderly!

In some indecision he wheeled and made for the door. Of a sudden he paused there. Straightening himself, he clicked his heels together in salute, like to any private. Instantly Rehnskiöld dropped into silence. The door was opened. An icy blast drove in. Then the cornet announced, in a shrill, high voice, as of a sentinel calling the camp to arms, " His Majesty."

No longer was the King the bedazzled and unwordly and undeveloped youth as of yore. Nought remained the same in him but the boyish figure with its narrow shoulders. His great cloak was shabby and dirty. The line now deeper about his arching upper-lip now added something of a simper to his face.

On his nose and both cheeks were frost-bites ; his eyelids were swollen red with constant cold ; the combed hair on his baldish head stood up like a serrated crown. He held his cap in both hands, and sought to hide embarrassment under some stiff and chilly ceremony.

Smiling on those present, he bowed to them severally ; each one bowed aye deeper in return. When he was come into the middle of the room, he stood still, bowing on both sides, but this time more hasty, apparently being full of what he had to say. Then for a little while he remained standing in deep silence. He stepped to Rehnskiöld, and, with a little short beck, took hold of him by the coat button.

" I pray you, your Excellency, give me two or three men as escort for a little outing of mine. I already have a couple of guardsmen with me."

" But, your Majesty ! The neighbourhood is over-run with Cossacks. Even now, it is full hazardous to ride from your Majesty's quarters into the town here."

" Oh ! Trifles ! Mere trifles ! Do as I say, your Excellency. One of the generals here, off duty, can also come along with us, and also take one of his staff "

Lewenhaupt made his leg. The King looked at him irresolutely, without a word, and remained in silence after Rehnskiöld had hastened outside. None present found it fitting to break in or bestir themselves. A good while after, the King once more inclined himself to each individually, then passed into the open.

" Now then, cornet, come with me," said Lewenhaupt, clapping him on the shoulder, for his usual good nature had returned. " It is the first time ye've seen his Majesty face to face? "

" Never had I thought of him as he is."

" He is never otherwise! He is overmuch of a King to order a man about ! " And the two went after his Majesty, who was clambering over wagons and fallen animals. His motions were nimble, never vehement, but measured and constant. Not for a single second did he forget his dignity.

At last, when he had forced a passage through the press about the town gates, he and his escort of seven men, sprang into their saddles. The horses slid about over the frozen bodies, some stumbling to the ground ; but Lewenhaupt's protest only made the King use his spurs more recklessly. The night long, Hultman in attendance had been reading or recounting Sagas to him. In the end, he had made the King merry by averring that, if God had not made him the Sovereign, he would have been a shy, stay-at-home his life through, thinking out as many fine verses as the

blessed Messenius himself in *Disa på Bollhuset*, and
above all, writing the most stirring epics. Now he
tried to think on Rolf Götrekson, that had aye ridden
first, at the head of his men ; but to-day could not
succeed in confining his thoughts within the narrow
circle of the Saga. The troubles, which of late had
thrust their claws into the body of his thoughts and
feelings, would not release their prey. The heated
countenances at the staff head-quarters still held with
him. Though long past the diversions of childhood,
he was engrossed with creating in imagination the
world of fantasy formed in olden times, and this
made him turn a deaf ear to the clamant notes of the
troubles around him, rendering him also distrustful of
any whose acuter hearing took perception of them.
As in former days, he scarce marked that now someone gave him the best-nourished and most powerful
charger of all, and the loaf with least salt in it, and of
a morning dropped a purse with five hundred ducats
into his pocket, and that, at the first insubordination,
the horse forming a ring about him, gave themselves
up to the death blows which himself provoked. So
it came to pass, that the troops greeted him with
sinister silence : and this misfortune had made him
suspicious, even of those nearest him. He took note
of the most prudent conversations, of the lightest dis-
approval, without betraying his attention ; but every
word remained in his recollection, gnawing at his
spirit. To him it was as if he were losing every hour a
right good officer, on whom he had had stable reliance :
and thus his heart was aye growing the colder. His

mortified ambition writhed and bled beneath the crushing weights of his ill-successes. But now, the further he left head-quarters behind, he breathed the lighter, the livelier.

Of a sudden, Lewenhaupt reined in his horse, and turned about, hoping to influence the King.

" My brave Ajax," said he, stroking his steaming horse. " 'Tis true, ye're an old crib-biter, but for all that, I will not have you founder without there is an end in view. But in the name of Jesu, fellows, follow the King. Who can ! " And noting the Cornet's uneasy look at his Majesty, he continued in a softer voice : " Rest easy, my lad. His Majesty never storms as we do. He is too much of a King to threaten and abuse any one."

The King held on as if he had noticed nothing. Wilder and wilder grew the rush over ice and snow, without prudence, without purport. Now he had but four of an escort. After some time a horse fell headlong, breaking its fore leg, and its rider, out of mercy, put a bullet through its eye. Alone and on foot he went in the cold to meet his uncertain fate.

At last, the cornet was the only one able to follow the King. The two were now among coppices and brushwood, where the horses could only go on at walking pace. Up on the hill, over against them, lay a dirty grey house, with narrow lattice windows, and a wall surrounding its courtyard. At that moment came a report.

" Where did that go ? " asked the King, looking about him.

" The little devil did not shoot amiss! He has missed my ear, but hit my hat-brim," answered the cornet, wholly ignorant of a subject's address to his King. He spoke with a soft Smaaland accent, and laughed unreservedly in contentment.

Intoxicated with the felicity of being companion to the King, to him more dear than all men living, he continued :

" We should go up, and beard them."

This greatly pleased his Majesty. In a leap he was on the ground.

" We will tie our horses to the bushes here," cried he, merrily, his cheeks a fiery red, " and then go and cut the man down, that shoots in such a manner ! "

Leaving the panting horses, they openly climbed the hill among the brushwood. Over the wall, round the courtyard of the house, there peered out some yellow Cossack heads, with locks hanging down, and features all twisted agrin, as they were those of decapitated malefactors.

" Look ! " cried the King, clapping his hands, " There they are, trying to close their rotten old gate, oh the fox-tails ! "

Instantly his eyes, so often listless, grew wide open, and gleaming with excitement. He drew his sword, and with both hands, raised it high above his head. Like to a young God, he stormed through the half-shut gateway. And at his side was the cornet, hewing and stabbing. Frequently was he almost cut down from behind by the weapon of the

King, whose right sleeve was scorched by a musket discharge.

Four men were overthrown in the gateway. A fifth, pursued by the King, fled into the court, a fire shovel in his hand. The King shoved his bloody sword in the snow, put two ducats on the Cossack's shovel, and cried with growing merriment. " It is no pleasure fighting with idiots like you, who never hit back, but take to your heels. Come back, will ye, when ye've bought yourself a serviceable sword ! "

The Cossack, who understood not, grabbed the gold, slunk alongside the wall towards the gate, and made off. As he scurried further and further away, they heard him calling on his comrades, strangely and complaining, " Ohahaa! Ohahaa!" The King trilled after him, as he were jeering at an invisible foe, " O ye Cossack mannikin ! O ye Cossack mannikin ! Only get ye together all your own little rogues."

Round the court of the house the walls were ruined and black, and from its depths came an unending, long-drawn moaning. In curiosity, the King opened the door of the house. It consisted of but one great half-lit room, and before the hearth lay a heap of blood-stained clothing, which the riflers had plundered from fallen Swedes. A sharp gust of wind slammed the door, and the King stepped further on to the stable. There, the strange noise was made explicable, for, tied to an iron ring in the wall, a white horse was lying, dying of hunger. An uplifted sword could not have kept back the King, yet the uncertain twilight in the place caused him to stay by the threshold, and he was trembling somewhat, for in the dark Karl became sorely afraid. Yet never he betrayed himself, but merely beckoned to the cornet. Down a steep stairway they went into a cellar. Round the creaking windlass of a draw well, here, a deaf Cossack, without a notion of danger, was driving with whip and bridle, a man in the uniform of a Swedish officer. When they had unloosed the prisoner, and bound the Cossack in his stead, they recognised Feuerhausen, the Holsteiner, Major in one of the recruited dragoon regiments. He fell on his knees.

" Your Majesty ! " he stammered in broken Swedish. " I believe not my very eyes ! My reconnaissance. . . ."

The King gaily interrupted him, turning to the cornet : " Bring up the two horses and stable them. It is not meet that three men ride on two horses, and therefore we remain here until the Cossacks come back. Then we take a third horse from them. You, sir, keep watch at the gateway." Hereupon the King stepped back into the house, and with his own hands, closed the door behind him.

The hungry horses, ravenously nibbling the bark off the bushes, were stabled, and the cornet took up his post. Wearily the hours slipped by. At the first of the darkening, the storm burst stronger, and by sundown the snow was whistling thick over the desolate stretches of ice-bound land. Cossacks, their faces a cadaverous yellow, emerged from behind the woody growths. Borne on the wind from afar echoed their call, " Ohahaa ! Ohahaa ! "

Then came Feuerhausen out of the stable where he had been sitting between the two horses to keep the cold out of his wound. He went up to the door.

" Your Majesty," he stammered, " the Cossacks gather in force. Soon it will be night. Allow us, myself and the cornet, to mount on one horse. If we stay here, this will surely be your Majesty's last night, which God forbid ! "

The King replied from within :

" It is as I have spoken. It is not meet that three men ride on two horses."

The Holsteiner shook his head, and went down to the cornet.

" That's your King, your accursed Swede ! In the stable, there, I easily heard how he is aye walking up and down, never resting a tittle. Aye, the bite of illness and the bite of conscience is there indeed. The Muscovite Tzar is like the father of a family among his subjects : he makes a pastry-seller his friend, and a low serving-lass he puts on his illustrious throne ; when he carouses, his habits are detestable, and he treats woman-kind *à la Français* ; but his first and last word is for Russia's good. King Karolus, he leaves his country a smoking ash-heap. He has not a single live friend, even among his nearest and dearest. He is more lonely than the poorest serf. He has not even a comrade to whom he could pour himself forth. Among fine folk and kept women, and periwigs, he wanders about like a ghost out of a thousand-year-old mausoleum—and for the most, ghosts do wander alone ! Is he something of a states-

man?—no head at all for the common-weal! Is he
a general?—all amiss! Never a care of the troops!
But to break down bridges, put gabions in place,
and clap hands over a captured standard and a pair
of kettle-drums, he can do that! No head for the
kingdom and his army, only for men!"

"Therefore we also can have a head!" answered
the cornet.

He walked swiftly up and down. By now his fingers
were so stiff with cold, that he hardly could keep a
grip on his unsheathed sword.

The Holsteiner drew the torn collar of his coat up
about his cheeks.

With deep sounding voice, and vigorous gestures,
he cried:

"King Karolus, he laughs in delight if the bridges
break, and men and beasts drown most miserably.
He has no heart at all! To hell with him! King
Karolus? He is nought but a little half-genius of
a Swede, that has strayed out into the world with
a blare of trumpets and much parade; but now
comes the break-down in the play, and all the pit
hisses!"

"And, even so, the Swedes go to death for him!"
replied the Cornet.

"Be not so heady, comrade! I myself have made
play, when of late ill luck came our way!"

"Willingly I listen to you, Major, but meantime
I am freezing. Would you not go up again, and
listen?"

The Holsteiner went upstairs and gave an ear.

On his return he said:

" He does nothing but walk about the room and sigh like a man of grievous, heavy heart. Now it aye appears to be, that his Majesty sleeps no more of a night! The mummer feels his part important no more, and of all tortures that is the worst—wounded ambition!"

" Then must it also be the last to make merry on. Durst I ask you to rub my hand with snow, it is numb!"

The Holsteiner did as desired, and turned again to the King's chamber.

His greyish moustache stood out all bushy. He beat himself on the forehead with both hands. He muttered, " Lord God! Lord God! Soon 'twill be too dark for us to return."

Called the cornet. " Good sir, durst I ask you to rub my face with snow. My cheeks are frozen. I'll not speak of the pain in my feet. Oh! oh! I can endure it no longer."

The Holsteiner took hold of his hands all covered with snow.

" Let me keep watch," said he. " At least for an hour!"

" No, no. The King has given order that I stay here by the gate."

" Ah, this King! I know him, believe me! I will answer for him. Speak of philosophies, and relate intrigues to him. He is aye amused to hear about lovers. Often he takes a sly look at the women when they are beautiful. But to him they exist only for his imagination, not for the lust of his flesh ; for that is beneath his dignity ! And he is so shy. If a woman, in truth, desires to have him at her feet, she herself must attack him, and act as she had fled to him for protection, and all others must work and agitate against the liaison. His most gracious grandmother has spoilt all by aye crying ' Marriage. Marriage.' Save for his man's face, he resembles the Swedish Queen Christina. Had the two sat on the throne, there would have been a neat little pair of them ! Ah, you Swedes. A man may ride his bent to the death, may ruin army, folk, and kingdom ; yet, after all this, he has a noble heart and soul, to your idea ; and is among all that is best ; and this only because his blood is something of a sluggard's in amorous intrigue. No more to me, now ! I know heroes of right noble heart and parts, who have been loved in all reality and passion by two and three different wenches or dames ; aye, and all in one and the same week, too ! "

" Yes, and so are we ! So are we ! But for Christ's sake rub my hand again ; and forgive my cries and groans."

Near by, in the gateway which was unclosable, lay the dead Cossacks, white as marble with the frost. The yellow heavens were become grey. And ever nearing, ever increasing, resounded the plaintive holloaing, "Ohahaa. Ohahaa." It was now that the King opened the door, and came down into the court. His riding in the wind had aggravated the pains in his head, from which he frequently suffered, and which

M

made his glance dull and spiritless. His face bore
traces of his endured loneliness. Yet immediately he
approached them, his mouth wore its wonted smile.
The grime from the musket discharge still besmutched
his temple.

" The wind has freshened," said he, drawing a loaf
out from under his coat.

He divided it into three, so that each had an equal
part. After this he took his cloak, and threw it round
the shoulders of the cornet. Confused at his own
action, he impetuously seized the Holsteiner by the
arm, and led him across the yard, whilst they munched
the hard bread.

Now or never, thought the Major. I must be clever
now, and seize the King's attention, and discreetly
give a word of advice.

" One could be in a worse plight," he began, still
munching. " Ah, yes, it all puts me in mind so
well of an intrigue once set ago near Dresden."
The King still retained his arm, so he lowered his
voice.

The tale was droll and piquant, and the King grew
inquisitive. But nevertheless the most obvious broad
allusions aye occasioned the same awkward inspirited
laughter. His Majesty listened to him like to one
desperate and nigh distraught, with need of immedi-
ate distraction.

When the Holsteiner warily began to turn the talk
on the present danger, the King again became earnest
and life-like.

" Mere nothing !—nothing ! " he replied.   " Not

worth a word if we only keep a good front when the blackguards assail us again ; all three of us but place ourselves in the gateway ; and look to ourselves with our swords ! "

In despair, the Holsteiner rubbed his forehead and changed the theme. He commenced to talk of the myriad stars twinkling overhead, and enumerated a rule for measuring their distances from the earth. Now the King gave him a better hearing. With acutely reasoned and ingenious questions he interrupted him, and to the given reason devised new conclusions with untiring gratification. One question succeeded another, and soon the conversation dwelt on the universe and the immortality of the soul, to come back once to the constellations in the heavens above, which were glittering bright by now. The King gave out what he knew about the sundial. He thrust his sword in the snow, and its point he set toward the pole star, so that they could read the time in the coming morning.

" Either," said he, " must the earth be the centre of the universe ; or that star standing over against Sweden. There is nought above Sweden.

Before the walls the Cossacks called to one another. But when the Holsteiner again sought to bring the talk on their dangerous proximity, straightway the King grew tongue-tied.

Said he :

" When morning begins to lighten, we ride back to Hadjatsk. By that time we will have seized a third horse ; then each of us can ride in his own saddle." And after he had said this, he retired into the house.

With quick steps the Major came down to the cornet. Half-turning to the King's door, he cried:

"Forgive me, cornet. We Germans do not weigh our words, when our wounds are smarting. I surrender, and leave the victory to you, for I, too, could die for the man up there. None have understood him who have not seen him. But surely you dare stay no longer out there in the cold?"

The cornet answered:

"No cloak has ever warmed me so gloriously as that I am now wrapped in, and I cast all my sorrows on Christ. But in God's name, Major, go back to the door and listen; the King might do injury to himself."

"His Majesty will not fall by his own sword, but yearns after that of others!"

"Now I hear his footsteps, hear them even down here! They grow aye quicker and wilder. He is so lonely. When I first saw him in Hadjatsk, and how he bowed, and bowed, and bowed again before his generals, I had but one thought: How lonely he is."

"Ay! And if this little Holstein man gets out of this, with his life, he will ever bethink himself of these footsteps we're hearing to-night. And this place he will aye name the place of the Mount of Olives."

The cornet nodded in assent.

"Go ye back into the stable, Major," he said, "and seek some rest and shelter between the mares. And there, too, ye can better hear the King, through the wall, and have a care of him."

Then he began to sing with loud voice:

> "In Thy mercy, oh tender Father."

The Holsteiner stepped over the yard, and into the stable, and himself shaking with cold voiced in tremulous tones:—

> "In all seasons put I my soul
> And all that in me is
> Within Thy custody."

"Ohahaa. Ohahaa," answered the Cossacks through the storm. And already it was late in the night.

The Major pressed himself between the two horses, and lay awake for a long time in a listening posture, till tiredness overcame him, and his head sank aside.

Towards the dawn of morning a tumult awoke him. He sprang out into the open. Already the King was down in the yard, and reckoning the hour of morning from the sword. But Cossacks were gathering in front of the gateway. Yet on marking the ever immoveable sentinel they took to retreat in a panic of superstition, bethinking themselves on all the rumoured spells wrought by Swedes against swordplay and bullets.

The Holsteiner gripped the cornet by the arm.

"What now," cried he. "Brandy, eh?"

But the same instant he let go. For the cornet was standing there, frozen to death, his shoulders against the gateway wall, his hands hard and fast round the hilt of his blade, and himself still wrapped in the cloak of his sovereign.

" Now," said his Majesty, drawing his weapon out of the snow, " we are but two men.   We can ride off now, each on his horse, as I said."   But with re-kindled hatred the Holsteiner stared him full in the face and stood stock-still as if he had heard not a word.

In the end he led out the horses; but his hands so shook and clenched themselves, that he scarce was able to fasten the saddle girths.   And with their swords and lances the Cossacks threatened to make fight.   Yet ever the Swedish sentinel stood on guard.

Impetuously the King swung himself up into his saddle, and went off at full gallop.   Unclouded was his forehead.   His cheeks flamed red.   Like the very sun's ray, his sword gleamed gloriously bright.

The Holsteiner looked at him.   Then his grim look softened, and with his hand at the salute he rode by the sentinel.

" That is but the joy," he muttered between his teeth, " of one hero over the rare death of another. My comrade, I do thank thee now."

CHAPTER XI.

A CLEAN WHITE SHROUD.

BENGT GETING, the dragoon, was pierced through the breast by a Cossack lance. His comrades had laid him down on a heap of faggots in the little wood near by; and here Pastor Rabenius administered the last sacrament to him.

The Swedes were now on the ice-covered fields before Wegerik. And out of the north a screaming wind was tearing the withered leaves off the trees.

"The Lord be with thee," said Rabenius in a tender and fatherly voice. "Are ye ready, Bengt Geting, to depart when this day's work is done?"

Bleeding to death, Bengt Geting lay there, motionless and with clenched hands and stark staring eyes. The skin of his bony, obstinate countenance was tanned so thick with the frost and the sun's rays, that the blue pallor of death was only apparent on his lips.

"No," answered he.

"Bengt Geting. It is the first time that I have ever heard ye utter a word."

Clenching his hands tighter, the dying man bit these lips of his that opened against his will.

"Surely, for once," said he slowly, "the most wretched and unruly man of all the Swedish troops will be allowed to speak."

He raised himself a little on his elbow. At that such a lamentable cry of agony escaped him that Rabenius knew not whether it came from tortured soul or body. So he set the cup on the ground, spreading his handkerchief over it, lest the fluttering leaves should fall into the brandy. He pressed his hands upon his forehead.

"And this," he faltered, "and this must I, a servant of Christ, behold from morn till night, and from one day after another."

On all sides the soldiers thronged forward betwixt the coppices, to look at the stricken man, and hearken. Their captain broke into hot anger. He thrust himself between them with drawn sword. Cried he:

"Bind a cloth over the fellow's mouth. He was aye the most mulish in the whole battalion. I am as human as the others, but must do my duty. I have a great number of new and untried recruits newly arrived with Lewenhaupt's command. Bengt Geting's groaning has put them in fear; and they refuse to advance. Why do ye not obey, there? Am I in command here?"

Rabenius took a step toward him. On his white full-bottomed wig there already lay as it were a wreath of yellow leaves.

"Captain," said he, "among the dying the servant of the Lord alone commands. Three years now have I seen Bengt Geting in rank and file; but until now, never have I seen him speak to any man. Now, when on the threshold to the judgment of God, none can force him to keep silent any longer."

"With whom should I speak?" the dragoon asked in all bitterness. "My tongue is as grown up and stricken with palsy. Weeks and weeks passed, and I never uttered one word. Nobody has, at any time, asked me about anything. It was only my ear which had to keep at the ready, for fear it neglected hearing. 'Go on,' we were bidden, 'through fen and snow. Go on.' There was nothing to say in reply."

Rabenius went on his knees, and gently took both hands in his.

"But now, Bengt Geting, ye should speak. Speak. Speak out. All are now gathered to hear ye. Of us all only you have the right to speak out freely. Have ye got a wife? or an old mother at home? Whom I should greet for you?"

"My mother let me starve, and put me to follow the sword. Since then never a woman has had a word to say other than, 'Get out of the way, Bengt Geting. Get out of the way. Get out! What want you with us?'"

"Then it is something at heart that you repent of?"

"I repent that when a child I did not jump into the mill-stream; and I am sorry, too, that when ye stood before the regiment and did exhort us to go on again aye in patience, I did not start out and fell ye with the butt of my musket! But will ye know then what

troubles me? Have ye never heard the baggagers
and out-posts say how in the moonlight they have
seen their dead comrades hobbling in throngs back to
the troops, and heard them cry, 'Greet my mother
for me.' They call them the Black Battalion. In that
Black Battalion I must also march. But the worst is
that I should be buried in my miserable rags and
bloody shirt. It is that which tortures me. A
common dragoon does not wish to be buried like to
the good General Liewen ; but I think on the comrades
killed at Dorfsniki : to each of them the King bade
be given out two boards for a coffin, and one clean
white shroud. Why should they be better off than
myself? In this unhappy time now, where a man
falls, there he lies. And I am sunk so deep in misery
that the only thing in the world for which I envy
all others is each his clean white shroud."

"My poor friend," Rabenius answered tenderly,
"in the Black Battalion, if ye believe truly therein,
ye are in right great company : Gyldenstolpe, and
Sperling, and Colonel Mörner already lay dead on the
field. And recall the thousands of others. Recall
the friendly Colonel Wattrang, who came riding up to
our regiment, and gave every man an apple, how he
is lying with the guardsmen and all the comrades
under the high road at Holofzin. And have ye in
mind my predeceaser, Niklas Uppendich, powerful
preacher of the Word, who fell, in his vestments, at
Kalisch. The grass is grown over his grave, and the
snow-storm swept over it, and no man can show
truly the place where he sleeps."

Rabenius bent lower over the dying man, and smoothed his forehead and hands.

"In ten or fifteen minutes, at most, you will have ceased to live. Maybe it is, that in these few minutes you can make up for what you have neglected in the past three years, if you turn them to right account. No more are ye one of us. Do ye not see your Pastor on his knee beside you, with bared head? Speak now, and tell me thy last wish, nay, command one. Think of one. The regiment stands in disorder by reason of you, while the others storm forward, or by now are on the scaling ladders. Fear have ye put into the young men through your death wound and agony; none but you can make amends. They are listening to you, Bengt Geting, and only you have the power to bestir them to advance. Bethink yourself. Your last words will long resound. Maybe in coming years they will be repeated at home before those who sit and roast their pears behind the stove."

Bengt Geting lay still. Into his eyes came an intense expression. Slowly he raised his arms as if in supplication.

He whispered:

"Help me, Lord, even to bring about this." Then he signified that he could but whisper, so Rabenius, putting his face close to his, heard him.

The Pastor beckoned the soldiers. But his voice was so tremulous, that scarce could he make himself understood.

"Bengt Geting has now spoken. It is his last wish that ye take him between you on your muskets, and carry him to his old place in the ranks, where he has marched in obstinate silence, day after day, year after year."

The advance was sounded, and to the bugles flaring Bengt Geting, leaning against the shoulder of a fellow private, was borne step by step over the battlefield, on towards the enemy. And after him followed the entire regiment.

Behind him walked Rabenius with uncovered head, and marked not that already Bengt Geting was dead.

" I will see to it," said he softly, "that ye get a clean white shroud.   Thou knowest, the King thinks himself not higher than the lowest of his soldiers. And he himself will be the same, one day."

CHAPTER XII.

POLTAWA.

ON the first of May, Field Marshal Rehnskiöld gave a supper. Colonel Appelgren was flushed and heated, and was rolling the bread into little pellets with his fingers. Cunningly he looked about him. All inquisitive he put the question :

" Maybe your Excellency can tell me why Poltawa should so suddenly be beseiged ? "

" His Majesty desires some amusement, till the Poles and Tartars come to his assistance."

" And yet we all know well that not a single one comes. Ah! Europe begins to forget our Court : our Court a la Diogenes, with its ministers of State scouring round, chancellors fighting, chamberlains killed, and with its seats of honour on tree-stumps. . . . Our Court with its Palace of canvas, and nothing but rice cakes and small beer on the Royal table."

" His Majesty would instruct himself in the science of laying a siege, and would enjoy camp life; so he prolongs the affair as long as he desires. There is no hurry! Poltawa is a paltry piece of fortification. To all evidence, 'twill surrender at the first crack of our guns."

Of a sudden the Field Marshal became silent, and let his fork fall.

" I do believe our folks are in some disorder out there, and defend themselves." Without, a continuous rolling of musketry was to be heard. All leapt to their feet. Rehnskiöld ran outside, and threw himself into the saddle, the others on his heels.

It was the nightly custom of the Russian sentinels on Poltawa ramparts, to taunt the Swedes, loud and vociferous, with yells of "Good bread! Good liquor!"

Now during this hubbub of theirs, Colonel Gyllenkrook, all unheard, had begun to open up his trenches, and placed a covering party therein. At the same time the King came galloping over the field, and speaking somewhat loud to the Adjutant General. Gyllenkrook begged of him to lower his voice, lest it give the alarm. But even as the Colonel spoke, the sentinels held their peace, and immediately after that their flares were set alight, and the firing broke out. Ascending fireballs threw their glare over the hillocks and on the grassy plain, gleaming also on the waters of the fast flowing Vorshla. Gyllenkrook's sappers fled from their spades and gabions; the covering party, at first beat back the sappers with the flat of their swords; in the end, they also began to retreat or throw themselves, stretched out on the ground. In this way, then the fusillade was begun.

" Behold, Sire," cried Gyllenkrook, standing behind a tree trunk, together with the King and the Little

Prince, "how a trifling affair can beget such a tremendous commotion! Once more may I suggest to your Majesty that you raise the siege? Our worn-out troops join in this entreaty, and all your unhappy subjects at home. Why are we not sent hither in winter? the town could then be taken with no trouble! But now its garrison is growing stronger every day, and the entire army of the enemy is on the march. We have but thirty pieces of cannon left. Our powder, too, often wet and redried, carries the ball short."

"Trifles! Mere trifles! For all that, we have shot through many balks thicker than a palisade."

"But, here, Sire, we must needs batter in many hundreds!"

"If one can be pierced, so can hundreds. In truth, it is the uncommon which we must achieve to win our fame and honour. Now we would show the sappers that they can work without the slightest danger." And with his broad-sword under his arm, the King walked over the field through a rain of musket-balls.

Behind him came the Little Prince. White-faced he was, and solemn as a stripling of olden times in festival procession to the sacrifice.

By the trenches two great stakes, like to posts, had been driven into the earth, and here the King remained, standing behind a pan of flaming pitch.

The Little Prince eyed him askance, his hand trembling as its fingers slid up and down the sword hilt. Then he climbed up one of the stakes, seated himself at the top, and let his arms dangle by his sides. A sergeant, Maarten Predikare by name, instantly mounted the other. Motionless, like two holy images of painted wood, by the Catholic's roadside, the two remained on guard behind their King. The infuriated Russians trained their culverins, cannons, and muskets upon the strange spectacle. The air flashed fire, whizzed and whistled as if beaten with whipthongs, blustered and thundered like a stormy blast; the ricochetting cannon balls threw high the sand and turf, and the solid earth shook like to a frightened horse. Splinters of wood and bits of stone flew thick about them.

"The King is there. They will kill him!" cried the soldiers; and, leaping forward, forced the sappers along with them.

Again spades were plied, and again the sappers tore up the sods. They delved holes for shelter. But there, in the glare of the burning pitch, stood he who, to his nobles and generals, was his Majesty; to the soldiers, a comrade; and who, at the same time, was a veritable knight of the road, king, and philosopher.

All that day sinister recollections had filled his heart. He thought of Axel Haard, whom he himself had unwittingly killed, and of dead Klinckowström, friend of his youth. He did not miss their company, but could not forget their blood-besmirched clothing. Now, as he heard the bullets, there awoke in him once more all the Heaven-storming bravado of his youth, and it silenced heavy thought. He had tasted the beaker of war to its very dregs: now every sip required a stronger seasoning. He took a colder enjoyment in his great, tumultuous victories, as they became the fewer. Yet sometimes he could speak bravely fine, of how that he purposed ruling over a great and extending dominion; but this was all to the end that his talk daily provided him with strong, fresh guardsmen. Never did he forget that any moment might be his last, and that the years of misfortune were come. Yea, how goodly rest i' the grave would be after an honourable death. It was something to have an end in view, and to feel that one had the strength to accomplish that end, yet to fail therein, and become a thing of derision because succour from others failed—that was even as the bitter frosty breath of the autumn of life. His fate he would challenge! He would show the world that still he was the Elect of God; if he were not, then would he fall, even as one of the commonest of his soldiers.

In the meanwhile, Maarten Predikare became so eager for fight, that he could sit still no longer. Who knew not Maarten Predikare, the incomparable sharp-shooter? His Majesty himself applauded him.

He snatched the musket off his back. Amidst that crackling fusillade he chattered and laughed most merrily. Levelling his piece, he let fly a shot at a shadow espied high up among some cherry trees in the distance. Down it dropped like a bird amid the branches.

The hunter's lust leapt up in Maarten, and he sprang down and ran to the place. An old man lay dead there.

N

A girl of nineteen was standing beside the body.

Said she, with never a tear, "It is father:" and looked Maarten Predikare full in the face. "We came out to pluck nettles, and were now on the way home. We heard the shooting; so father climbed up to look about. The cherry trees are his own!"

Maarten shook his head, took off his hat, passed his hand over his hair, and at length seated himself on the ground.

"God forgive me . . . the old man never did aught to me . . . dear child . . . ye cannot understand: . . . but I have a ducat in my pocket, here, take it! Lass, I am a hunter, ye understand; a real born old hunter! In early times I had my little place at home, and my wife that aye cuffed me because I would never handle a spade.—D'ye know, now, what a spade is?—But I sat in the woods, and listened to the notes of the blackcock. Hear now, what I say! One morning I took my gun and my dog, and went my way out, out into the wide world."

The girl examined the ducat in the glare of the fires. He took her upon his knees, and lightly stroked her cheeks.

"The very first day, after I had left her, I shot my dog! The second day I gave all my guelders to a woodcutter, who showed me the way; then I had nothing left me!"

"Can I buy things with this?"

"Ay, of course you can! When I became a soldier, then, and they gave me a musket, you can just believe what happened: I became a hunter again! But God

have mercy. . . . Every night, now, at the
darkening, ye must come softly to me, and then ye'll
get the half of my ration and all I can scrape together
for you."

He looked at his gun lying among the grass, then
got up and went away leaving it lying there.

"The lass surely cannot know that it was I that
fired the shot, and she must never know! I am a
Judas, the slayer of an innocent man. Do no murder.
Do no murder." And with his hands on his forehead,
Maarten staggered across the field. In time he came
to d'Albeduhl's Dragoons, who were lying round a
fire of wood, and reading the prayer-book. Here, he
sat him down, and also read the Holy Scrip; and in
the end, began to pray aloud, and to hold forth. . . .

"What is there fresh?" the soldiers asked next
morning of Brakels, the red-haired sutler.

A little omniscient man was he. In his grey smock
he was standing amid his pots and pans, and the
lines of dangling clothes.

"Fresh? I' faith Maarten Predikare has got sun-
stroke in the middle of the night, and is fit for nought
else but the mad-house! Bare-headed and all he is
down there by the water, groaning and praying, and
making much noise. When the preaching craze
takes him, it's clear he has killed his man!"

Lowering and all in silence the soldiers got their tin
bowls, now scarcely half filled with victuals.

"Food or death! Why do they not let us storm
the town before it is too late?"

"The King tries, by carrying forward the trenches;

N—2

Gyllenkrook has to work night and day. Hark ye, listen to Maarten Predikare down at the water side. In these times, now, with all this praying and psalm droning about us, 'twill warm the heart again when once the Field Marshal comes bellowing at us."

Maarten Predikare, at the darkening, furtively made off to the cherry trees. The girl was awaiting him. Her glossy flaxen tresses were almost white, and her face was grave. He had his ration with him. He also gave her the last kopeck in his pouch, for leave to kiss her on both cheeks.

" Is your mother living? " She shook her head.

" What do they call you? "

" Dunja ! "

He wished to kiss her again ; but she withdrew herself from his hold.

" Give me a kopeck, first ! " was her cry.

He went to the camp and begged kopecks from everyone he met.

Said he to himself:

" I'll protect that lass when we storm the town. She is like a little princess ! Something out of my pay I will lay by for her, too, so some day she'll have a little dowry when she marries. Why should she not marry ? Certainly, certainly ! I have one wife at home ! and another one here, among the baggage ! I am moreover a murderer. Of a certain a little princess must get married ! "

He had procured a copy of St. John's Gospel, so now he set himself to read out of it to d'Albeduhl's dragoons.

The spring laughed in all its bravery of green on the hilly stretches of country as far as Vorshla down the yellow river; but the Swedes only looked Poltawa ward. Upon an acclivity amidst the woods the town peered out, with its white monasteries, wooden towers, palisadoes; and its walls upon which young and old, women and children, piled high a breastwork of bags of earth, wagons, boughs, bundles of faggots, and puncheons.

"What is there fresh? Are we never to be led against the enemy?" the soldiers asked the sutler.

"The enemy is courteous enough to come and meet us," he answered, drying his sweaty brows. "To-night I listened to the cannon. Most of the cracks are not roaring out from here: we have no more shot left except what the Zaporogs pick up off the field. The Tzar's whole army, too, is already on the far side of the river!"

Then General Major Lagerkrona came galloping along, and calling out that the King was wounded in the foot. Beside the King's ambulance sat the Field Marshal, showing him, in his note-book the position of the seventeen redoubts which the enemy had already begun to throw up at Pietruska.

"What's new?" the men growled day by day.

"They have nothing to offer us; I am the richer, then!" replied the sutler, and described a circle with his ladle on the green turf-floor. "The King's foot is mortifying; all the brandy is drunk; the bread is eaten; I have but some porridge for you, to-day, and then the groats are also finished. The

enemy have beaten us; they will force us to retreat.
Hell take it, that we Swedes have to stand such hard
fortune ! "

He stamped on the ground, put the ladle to his
jowl, and, like an assassin, took aim in the direction
of the King's booth. But the trusty soldiery turned
away their eyes, notwithstanding their sore hunger
and suffering.

" Do no murder," whispered Maarten Predikare
with uplifted arm.

So the month of May passed away, and the rays of
the June sun streamed through the tent-tops. The
troops sat in line, plaiting wreaths for the May-poles.
But they never uttered a word. They were thinking
on the green reaches of pastures in their own dear
land, on their homes, on the wide, wide stretches of
sandy field.

On Sunday, a little before vespers, Maarten slunk
off to the plantation. For a few kopecks little Dunja
handed him a basketful of the first half-ripened strawberries ; and he divided them with her. He stroked
her small hands ; and played with her, carrying her
like a little child ; but never could he get her to
laugh ; aye kept she a grave countenance. Yet for
his last three kopecks she suffered him to kiss her
cheeks.

When he returned to the camp, he found all in
commotion and uproar. Officers were inspecting the
equipment of the troops, and examining swords, some
of which were ground so thin, that they more resembled
scythes than serviceable blades. Brakels, the sutler,

was getting his empty cooking-pots together. The King had decided to offer fight.

On the seat of turfs before the King's booth, the leaders were already sitting, to receive orders and instructions. There sat melancholy Lewenhaupt, with his big, clear eyes, and a small Latin lexicon between the breast buttons of his coat. There sat mighty Creutz, his hands resting on his sword-hilt; and there Sparre and Lagercrona carried on a lively conversation. Colonel Gyllenkrook was standing at a table, bent over his drawings; so engrossed was he, that he paid no heed to the others; only, now and then he brushed a sandfly off his beloved plans. Leaning over a little behind him, and in his worst mood, stood the Field Marshal, with his sharpish snub nose and girlish mouth contracted and purple lipped.

The march took place at eventide with colours cased and silent drums. For a while the King's litter was set down in a little wood in front of the guards. Then it could be heard from the scene of the siege how the enemy, hitherto cooped up, were now battering down their palisadoes, and were busily building a scaffold. The host of the Karolineans, once so arrogant, were now so short of powder and ball, that they could take into action only four cannon. And when they heard the crashing of the enemy's axes so near, scarred old veterans were seized with so pricking a dread, that they besought their companions for ducats to buy brandy, and in this wise win courage; but to no avail!

The moon was now dropped. The horses stood

saddled, and the men with their carabines or muskets in their hands. A loud murmuring arose from a regiment of infantry as their pastor served Communion. The gloom was so thick, that he had to feel before him with the left hand to fetch the cup to the mouths of his communicants. Round the ambulance, by the side of which the King had thrust in his sword, the generals had laid themselves down for a little, covered with their cloaks; and Piper sat on a saddle, his shoulders against the stem of a tree. Thinking to drive away sullen thoughts, they all engaged in a philosophical discourse with his Majesty. There he sat, then, in a circle of wise and learned men, as a master in his school; and Lewenhaupt, the true old Roman read aloud Latin verses.

When he came to an end he took a flaring torch from the lackey, and illumed the countenance of the King, whose head was fallen to the side. Piper and every one of the generals rose up; their enmity they let slip; so beautiful was the spectacle of the slumberer to them. His hat lay on his knee; the covering was spread over the bandaged foot; his thin, fever-stricken face, frost-bitten on the nose and cheeks, seemed smaller, harder, and more inflexible in expression than afore, but, sallow and wrinkled, it already bore the marks of premature old age. A painful expression came and went about the corners of his mouth. 'Twas like the King was dreaming.

The King of the Karolineans dreamed he saw an interminable row of laughing, grinning men hurrying by, and holding their hands before their faces to hide their merriment from him. Some were of a bright green, and some blue, and some red ; and when they laughed they were full of flame, like to burning lant-horns. At last a tall man ranged past, mounted on a dark chestnut steed, and clothed over all in soiled black taffeta. " Out, out with you, you lame, sallow-faced Swede ! " cried he, loudly laughing down at him. " On this very spot, three hundred years ago, the hordes of Tamerlane drove back the whole army of the West. What will you do to me and my myriads ? You, with your few worn-out regiments and your four pieces of cannon ? Of a truth my men are but wild thieves and vagabonds ; are of no more account to me than nails are to a plank ; but, many, many such nails have I. A great ship I build, that is to last for thousands of years ; and to-day I am still the same who once stood on the wharves at Saardam ; nought but a simple joiner man. Millions and millions will call blessings on my work." And the King would that he could answer, yet was tongue-tied.

It was just then that Lewenhaupt, on bended knee, with bared head, was lightly touching his Majesty on the shoulder.

" Sire ! Sire ! Day dawns ! And I implore the protection of God on your royal person and on the work of your hands this day."

When the King opened his eyes the morn was already glowing red between the trees. Instantly he clutched his sword, but on marking the many about him, Nordberg, the bearded chaplain, and all the others, his expression straightway altered ; and he bowed with his usual friendly reserve.   Yet the vision held in his soul : and it was to him as if the rest, also, had seen it.

"My people," said he, "is too small to establish an extending dominion, but strong enough to fashion great men.   What is a dominion?   A contingency of fortune! a wide-spreading possession, with fortified frontiers!   And, O Tzar, hadst thou power over millions but none over thyself, what then?   For the Lord our God can so order it in one, that he may care but little for the State and the things of State, but more for the individual man in himself.   If I defeat you, O Tzar, thy mighty craft takes fire, and is turned into a heap of ashes ; but if ye beat me and mine, ye consummate merely the triumph of my personal task of self."

Lewenhaupt plucked at Creutz's sleeve.

"Dear brother," said he in dejection, "sinister forebodings will not leave me.   Will we all ever again stand together under God's open heavens?   Do ye hear how the Field Marshal, behind there, curses and raves at the Uppland men?   Gyllenkrook durst not once go near him.   Even you have some hesitation.   And see how Piper regards us with haughty looks!"

"The Swedes aye measure each other with such looks.   And therefore will they be overthrown one day, and their name blotted from out the book of nations. Our children will live over the hour of it all in ten or twenty ballads.   What takes place to-day is but the beginning!"

"The Lord forgive you for your words!   Never

have I seen such glorious heroes 'fore God as the
Swedes; and never a nation so entirely without distrust of the King's will and his heavy hand. But his
Majesty is now too ill to hold the men together,
although he is as confident as a young cornet. At
his birth he got that lightheartedness which the Gods
give their darlings: but now ——"

"Now?"

"Now he has recourse to an impenetrable self-
reserve and despair, like to all beloved of the Gods
when forsaken by them."

Lewenhaupt firmly pressed his hat on his head, and
drew his sword. But once more he turned to Creutz.

"Maybe it is that men like myself," he said, "with
my care for the troops, and Gyllenkrook with his com-
passes and all his palisadoed redoubts, have never
understood him aright. Thou and thy sword have
ever given him blind obedience. Ah, I would that it
is granted to us all this day to accomplish his mission;
for I prophesy that he who lives at even will miss his
comrades, gone by then into the bliss of the Kingdom
of Heaven." And Lewenhaupt went off to his infantry. By now the horse were in the saddle.

At open break of day they saw the battlefield before them. It was black, for the ground had already
been fired. A mere waste place of ashes it was, without flower or stubble, and stretching far over to disappear between groves of trees on the farther steppe.
It was so flat, that ammunition wagons could travel
easily over every part.

Before the hugest of the Muscovite redoubts, a

horseman clad in scarlet came spurring out, and fired a pistol. At this the enemy rolled loud their drums behind the fortifications, on which numberless troops, standards, culverins, and field-pieces were to be discerned. Immediately there was clashed in reply the marches of all the Swedish regiments, each in its turn.

Dauntless Axel Sparre and Karl Gustavus Roos, leapt forward with their battalions, and stormed the fieldworks. Horses snorted, accoutrements clattered, carabines and broad-swords clashed. Dust and ashes swirled up, covering the trees so thick that the foliage disappeared. Creutz, with the left wing, was dispatched by the King to reinforce victorious Sparre : and behind the works the enemy's cavalry were routed over the swamps toward the Vorshla. On the other side Lewenhaupt thrust forward with his foot, stormed two redoubts, and then disposed himself to carry the enemy's camp at the point of the bayonet. Here the consternation was tumultuous and great, and the women-folk commenced to yoke the horses into the baggage wagons. But the Tzarina, a tall woman, in the twenties of life, full-breasted, with a white forehead and high-coloured cheeks, never stirred ; calm and steadfast, she remained without, among the bandages and water flasks beside the wounded.

The generals, in the meantime, were gathering round the King's stretcher, some little way off the East Gotha regiment, and alongside a morass. A halt was called, and with bared head and bended knee, some began already to congratulate his Majesty, and desire a further advance.

While Hultman, the attendant, was filtering marsh water, collecting it in a silver cup, the King said:

"Major General Roos has got surrounded, so the Field Marshal has held back the other troops; but Lagercrona and Sparre are sent to the relief, and soon he ought to be here."

The Swedish army had to remain here for some time. But speedily Sparre came back, splashed with blood, and reported that, the enemy being in great force, he was not able to cut his way through. So now the troops were marched hither and thither, their officers not knowing where to place them. And in the lost time the Russians gathered fresh courage.

Then Lewenhaupt set himself in motion towards the little wood held by Creutz's Dragoons, and gave the word for the infantry to advance in line. None knew who had issued the order. Beside himself with rage, the Field Marshal galloped to the King's stretcher, which was being borne alongside the Life-guards.

"Did your Majesty command Lewenhaupt to advance in line upon the enemy?"

His disrespectful tone astonished the King. In a flash, it became evident to him how his very nearest favourites regarded him with weariness and indifference.

"No!" he answered with hesitation; but he flamed red. And all knew he lied.

With this, the last spark of regard and trust was extinguished in the furious and enraged Field Marshal. Because of his love for the truth, to him the far-famed

King was instantly degraded into a common soldier, that, behaving like a crass-headed lout, proffered a clumsy lie. No second thought took the Field Marshal. The moment of rupture was come. He controlled himself no longer, but gave way to the animosity and mistrust nourished by all in the past months. He burned to be able to punish, to humble, and to avenge himself. Now he could not act as if he believed the untruth, nor, no more would he use the accustomary address to his Majesty.

"Aye, aye," cried he, down from horseback, "the King is always doing this ! By God, I wish he would hand the command over to me." And with that he turned his back on his Majesty.

The King sat motionless on his ambulance. He had been put to shame in the face of the entire army. Through his nervousness and antipathy to wordy strife, he had been drawn into his untoward and sorry cowardice. His own folk had heard him lie like to any knavish baggager, and further without more prevarication, he could not take back his words. What he was suffering, as a man, from his humiliation was more intolerable than if he had lost his throne. His wish now was to leap up, throw himself on horseback, and ride thence with his men, the common soldiers, who still believed he was the Elect of God ; but the pain in his foot and grievous weakness kept him fettered. Hotly flushed were his cheeks ; but now it was with the fever of his illness ; and for the first time his sword shook violently in his hand, which now he scarce could lift up.

" The litter to the front," was his cry. " The litter to the front."

Gyllenkrook cried in passion to him, " The horse is not yet pushed forward.   Is it possible, the fight will only now begin ? "

" Now they advance," replied the King, all harassed. " The enemy is also throwing his foot forward."   So. then Gyllenkrook, commending his Majesty to the protection of the Almighty, threw himself into the saddle, and spurred on to the Guards, who had already advanced and fired the first salvo.

The Swedish field badge was a piece of straw on their headgear.   Through the furious crashing of cannon and clamour of battle, and blaring of trumpets and hautboys, and thudding of drums and rattling of kettle-drums, the war cry of the Swedes rang continually, " God with us.   God with us."   In the thick of the press, and on the plain, old campaigners encountered each other, and called out a last farewell ; or near relations, once boon companions at the feast and merry makings.   Where the space ranged wider, the captains, and lieutenants, and ensigns were marching in front of their battalions, pale-faced, but keeping time with the music, as though they were on parade in the Castle-yard at old Trekronor.   But the hands of the men were clenched tight over their empty cartridge boxes.

Under fire from the redoubts, the Guards advanced in close order, their muskets shouldered.   On nearing the enemy, they furiously gripped the useless pieces, and fixed bayonets.   But the dust and the gunpowder

tinted friend and foe alike grey ; the green tunics of
the enemy were not to be distinguished from the
Swedish blue, and Swede raised the sword against
Swede.

In the front of Kruses' Dragoons, Cornet Dveckselt
dropped from his horse, with a bullet in his body,
and the colours in his arms. Ridderborg, Captain
of horse, who that morning had witnessed his
gray-haired parent fall among the Guards around the
King's litter, was carried senseless out of the hand-to-
hand melée. Colonel Torstenson fell at the head of
Hyland's Regiment ; Lieutenant Gyllenbögel had a
bullet wound through both cheeks : daylight streamed
through them. In the thicket behind the Schonen
Dragoons, Captain Horn writhed about, severely
wounded in the right lung ; his trusty servant, Daniel
Lidbom, had clasped him to him, and was drying
his beady forehead. The cavalry man, Per Windropp,
sat his horse, dead, with the fringes of a torn company-
colour in his hands ; Lieutenant Pauli, thinking him
to be nought more than wounded, asked him for his
field-flask. Leading the Kalmar Regiment, Colonel
Rank fell, hit in the heart ; Major Lejonhjelm lay
with both legs shot away ; and beside the corpse of
Lieutenant-Colonel Silfversparre, Ensign Djurklo
fought with broken sword to save the colours, until
he, too, sank dying. Around him lay half of the
non-commissioned officers, and half of the company,
like as it had been a guard of honour. The Jönköping
Regiment, first at the redoubts, took its wounded
Colonel with it ; and when Lieutenant-Colonel Natt-

och-Dag and Major Oxe lay in their blood, Captain
Mörner took command. Before him, stretched on
the soil, lay the Ensign Tigerskiöld, bleeding from
five wounds, his face buried in his hands, and
supporting himself on his elbows. Hardly the fourth
part of the regiment could wield a weapon.

It was then that the Field Marshal came galloping
over the field, and roared in great anger to Mörner:

"Where the devil are the officers of this regiment?"

"They lay there, wounded or dead."

"Why the hell then, are ye not lying there also?"

"No! The prayer of my old mother has placed
me in the shelter of God, and so I still live, and have
the honour to take command over this regiment,
which has aye done its duty with honour, and aye
will do. . . . Keep steady, men. Keep steady."

Already Colonel Wrangel lay dead and unrecognis-
able, and his men strove in vain to seize hold of him
under his arms and get him on his feet. Colonel
Ulfsparre, leading on the West Gotha Regiment, fell,
his hands pressed over his heart, and his Major, reck-
less Sven Lagerberg, tumbled backwards to the
ground, hit with a musket bullet. The whole army
of the enemy charged in his direction. He heard the
trampling of horses and the clattering of the ammunition wagons. Between the stiffening corpses and
moaning wounded he was forced into the mud and the
ashes, was trampled on and bruised, until, at last, a
wounded dragoon put him on his horse and haled him
forth to the baggage.

Still fluttered the beloved, shot-riddled old colours

O

above the furious sea of men. But now they were rising and falling. Their stuff got more tattered; their staves broken; till at last they began to sink and disappear one after the other.

The Uppland Regiment, most of the men of which were drawn from the heart of Sweden, out of the old-time home in the Mälar valley, was in the last throes. The colours, with the cross-crowned apple in the corner, were wrenched away from the clenched hands of their fallen bearer. Their Colonel Stjernhöök was struck down beneath Cossack spears, and swords, and musket butt-ends, while murmuring, " Now is the time come when we must cry, Father, it is ended." Lieutenant Colonel von Post and Major Anrep fell almost side by side. Captains Gripenberg and Hjul-hammer, and Lieutenant Essen, and the three boyish ensigns, tall and beardless, Flygare, Brinck, and Düben, lay in the last breath of death.

" Stand fast, men. Stand fast! " cried officers and men alike; and fell down the one on the other, so that with the dead, and their torn clothing, and the turf, and sand, a mound accumulated which served the living as a breastwork. Whistling bullets, grenades, grape and canister shot stormed down. The atmosphere was so dense now with smoke and dust, that scarce could one see a horse-length away.

The Swedes began to waver. Lewenhaupt drew his holster pistols and levelled them at his own troops. Threatening them, he yelled :

" Keep your ground, men, in Jesu's name! I see the King's litter."

" If he is here, we will stand fast," answered the soldiers. And they yelled to one another, as if to overmaster their own sweaty blood-besmutched limbs, " Stand men. Stand firm. God with us."

Yet, despite all, were they driven back step by step.

The Swedish horse were repelled, till in the end, their hands and faces all hacked and hewed, they turned about their horses, man for man, in wild flight. Through the smoke they saw the King. He was lying on the ground among his fallen Guards, bearers, and attendants, hatless, and supporting himself on his elbows : his wounded foot high up on the wrecked ambulance, over which some had spread the blood-flecked cloak of Oxehufvud, the dead Guardsman. Blackened was his rigid face with gunpowder ; but his eyes were gleaming.

He stammered, " Swedes ! Swedes ! " And many among the fleeing horse drew rein on recognising that voice once more, for it came to them that if they escaped they must needs hear that awful and solitary calling anew when they lay dying.

The King could not arise of himself, but they lifted him upon their crossed lances, like to a doomed and irresolute sick person. Anew the bearers were shot down. Yet even in that moment, as, all bleeding, they stumbled on their knees, they threw out their arms to keep him from falling. Then Major Wolffelt lifted him on his horse, himself instantly to be struck down by the pursuing Cossacks. His Majesty's foot, set across the neck of the horse, was bleeding heavily, and its bandage trailing on the ground. A

cannon ball from the field works took a leg off the
horse; but the Guardsman Gierta put the King on
his own nag, mounting the three-legged one himself.
It was only through their desperate and furious exer-
tions, that the cavalry in a ring round his Majesty
could keep back the pursuers.

Meantime Gyllenkrook was scouring over the field,
trying to rally the soldiery. But this was their
answer: " We all are wounded, and our officers killed."
Then he fell in with the Field Marshal, who came
pelting behind him; and now on this day of reckoning no more heed was given him. It was in an
insulting manner Gyllenkrook called out to him:

" D'ye hear, your Excellency, how the firing still
holds on our left wing. Some squadron there, then,
has captured the position. Give them further orders,
do ye!"

" All is lost! Some obey me well, taking to their
heels; but few with their hearts," replied Rehnskiöld,
riding off aye the more to the left.

At the same time Gyllenkrook saw Piper with his
chancellery making off to the right. Had the two
spoken together? He cried to them that they were
riding from the foe. But they never turned themselves about. Gyllenkrook beat his hand on the
pummel of his saddle; for straightway he perceived
the measure to be full: nought save death or captivity
now awaited him.

Behind him there was no longer a stretch of open
country. Out of the ground an immense and moving
forest was now shot up; but the tree trunks were

men, and the boughs weapons. It broadened out.
Filling the whole landscape o'er, it marched without
ceasing, over the wounded and dying: it was the
army of the Tzar, coming to take possession, and
establish his sovereignty and authority for centuries.

Nearer and nearer there sounded a sacred hymn,
melancholy and deep chanted. Slowly and step by
step, as if in a funeral procession, the Imperial Standard was borne onward between swinging, smoking
censers, and high above the heads of thousands and
thousands again. There was to be noted on its silken
woof the genealogy of the Tzar, and, higher, under the
Trinity, was his likeness.

.   .   .   .

At the baggage the fugitives were gathered round
their King. He had bandaged his foot, and cleansed
his face somewhat of the grime of battle ; and was
now sitting in a wagon painted blue, beside Haard,
the injured Colonel.

" Where is Adlerfelt, the Chamberlain ? " he enquired.

Those around answered him : " He was struck
down by a cannon ball, close behind your Majesty's
litter."

At the same time, the Dal Regiment came by,
broken and in great disorder.

" Dalecarlians," cried the King, " where is your
Colonel, Siegeroth, and Major Svinhufvud, and
where the mighty Draken, that fought so bravely
before the redoubt ? Henceforth he must have a
regiment of his own."

" All are dead."

" Where is the Little Prince, and Piper, and the Field Marshal ? " And they standing around shook their heads, and looked at one another.

Should they tell him, for once, the entire truth? On this day of judgment should they discover to him all his isolation ? Should they tell him that she, the sister dearest to him, Hedwig Sophia, had lain for one half year in her coffin, unburied ? Not a man of them all durst have the courage.

" Prisoners," they replied, after some hesitation.

" Prisoners ! Prisoners to the Muscovite ? Then better the Turks ! Forward." His Majesty was deathly pale, but spoke in composed, almost triumphant, voice ; the same smile as ever was on his lips.

A grey-haired soldier among the Dalecarlians whispered to his comrades :

" In all fair truth, I have not seen him so happy and young since that day at Narva, when we went out with Steinbock. To him, this day is a day of victory ! "

The wagon rolled away. And at the head of his disorderly, unruly, fleeing host of loud-mouthed land-rakers, camp-followers, cursing and blaspheming, cripples groaning and moaning loudly, and lame, hobbling horses, the King of Sweden moved off with colours flying and drums abeating as if he had won his most triumphant victory.

. . . .

The last salvoes on the field were fired about two o'clock. After that a hush lay on the plain

where the last Cossacks of Mazeppa and numberless
Zaporogs were spitted alive on stakes. The habi-
tations and mills were burnt down; the woods
destroyed; the fallen were covered with ashes and
earth, and, stark staring, they all lay there as if
looking back from another world on their past years
and on the living.

A captive pastor and some soldiers were roaming
about seeking for the bodies of their own folk. They
dug a deep grave; and in the darkness of that fine
June night the service for the dead was softly murmured over it, in the speech of the distant home-land.
The tomb was then filled, to become overgrown in
time with the bent and the prickly thistle. For
these last hundred years the wind of the steppe
moans over it, down there in the gloomy stretch of
morass named by the Russians " The graveyard of
Sweden."

When one of the chaplains found Wetzel, the
Lieutenant-Colonel who had died together with his
two sons, he lifted up the empty covers of a prayer-
book lying on the ground beside the Colonel. They
were emblazoned with Wetzel's family bearings.

" Thou art the last of your line," said he ; " and, to-
day, many families are blotted out : Galle, Siegeroth,
Mannersvärd, Rosenkiöld, von Borgen. . . . And
now, while in the name of my mourning, stricken
country, I rend these arms off these covers, I destroy
the escutcheons of you all."

In front of the redoubt, where the fight had raged
most fierce, a multitude of corpses were thrown to-

gether in a heap ; but the rest were left strewn about
the plain. The air soon became filled with the ex-
halations of rot and decay, and with countless carrion
crows. With the deepening night silence fell dreadful
over the great immensity of graves ; only the wounded
broke it ; calling continually for water. Those of
them that were worst mutilated only made supplication that some one would take pity on them and give
them the death blow ; or trailed themselves to a dead
horse, tore the pistol out of the holster, and took their
own life, after they, with trembling lips, had besought
God's blessing on all at home, and repeated the Lord's
Prayer. Then a dragoon, stricken unto death, began
to speak great words of comfort, thanking the Almighty for the honourable death vouchsafed him. He
repeated the collect of burial over himself and his
comrades, and three times he took some earth into
his hand and besprinkled his bosom : " From the
dust art thou taken, and unto the dust wilt thou
return." All enrapt, he held forth concerning the
Resurrection, and in the end voiced loud and with
much cheer a burial psalm. Under the starry heavens
of that night it was responded to by twenty or thirty
voices in the distance.

Maarten Predikare, creeping without dread over the
field, continued the psalm when the dragoon became
silent. Then he took note of an old hag nearing him,
a torch in her hand ; and behind her a file of peasants
dragging long carts, which they were loading with
clothes and all sorts of plunder.

An ensign, not yet dead, would not suffer them to

steal a necklet of his, with a small silver cross to it.
With all his strength he resisted ; but they felled
him with a pitchfork. At this Maarten Predikare
approached. Cried he in a low voice, " Do no murder.
Do no murder."

Then among the marauding females he recognised
once more his Dunja, his little Dunja. His whole
countenance altered. Half like to a father, half like
to a bashful lover, he stretched forth his arms to
her.

She stared at him, and burst into idiotic laughter.

" It is the beastly Swede," cried she, "that bribed
me with money for cherries and kisses." And she
sprang at him like a cat.

His earrings she tore away, so that the blood
trickled down both sides of his neck. He fell. The
women beat him, and rent the clothes off his body.
They found his Epistle of St. John, and strewed the
pages about like to feathers of a plucked fowl. They
pulled off his top-boots and tattered stockings. But
when he marked that his little Dunja grabbed the
pitchfork, he tore himself loose, with all the force of
upstart hatred, and fled away in his shirt over the
dying and wounded.

" Not even the trust of an innocent heart is granted
to us any longer," he murmured, mounting a lame
horse that had come close to him in the night. "God
has forsaken us. Judgment is fallen on us. All is
ended ; and the whole world is dark."

For two nights and two days he rode on, and the
lagging wounded directed him. The fugitive Swedes

he found again on a neck of land between Vorshla
and the shining Dnieper, that broadened here into a
sea between its low banks overgrown with trees,
thickets, and reeds. The Russian was close upon
them to landward. But when the outposts descried
Maarten in his bloody shirt, and riding the saddleless
horse, they sprang aside in terror ; they only fired
when he was already past.

The sun burning fierce, the wounded and invalid
were bedded under the woody growths at the water's
edge. The generals were standing together, con-
versing.

Lewenhaupt turned in sadness to Creutz.

"With the King a captive," said he, "the Swedes,
to a man, will go home, and give up their last stiver
to get him ransomed. We bear the responsibility.
This war is like to a game of chess, in which all is to
protect the King. On my bended knees I have
implored him to allow himself to be ferried over, but
he thrust me away, saying he had weighty matters to
think on."

"You speak to him as ye were speaking to a gouty
statesman. Above all, talk not to him as to a young
man, but talk ye to him as if to a stripling who stands
with pride on his manhood."

Creutz neared the King's wagon, violently brandishing his gloves, as if he intended to hit him on the
forehead ; but the King's clear, steady eye straightway put him in confusion.

"Your Majesty is busy thinking ? "

"I fight but poorly with the pen, so I have re-

course to thought. I would make my last testament,
and arrange the succession. And then, should it go
amiss with me, if I remain on the field, I will be
buried in my shirt, like to any common soldier, on the
spot where I fall."

Creutz twisted and tugged at his gloves. Like
to his fellows, he was overmastered, and˄he had to
incline his head.

"Sire, I am not one of those that call on God to
let them live, for right well do I apprehend the dearest
wish of a hero. The bullet intended for your Majesty
may reach you. No! No! In Jesu's name! But,
Sire, you may not stay long in the saddle to-day.
God forgive my words, but your Majesty must suffer
himself to be carried about like to some poor,
miserable wretch, and when the last of us is dead,
you, Sire, must needs remain behind all alone, and
fall into captivity."

"Not only should a man stand one against five,
but he should be able to stand against the whole
world.

"True! True! But devil take it, we common
comrades of the uniform are not strong enough for
that! One against all: that is one against the entire
world. It needs men of wholly another sort ; we are
such weak folk, that we have nought but swords for
our protection! Now, after I, in all simplicity, have
placed the situation even as it is, I beseech your
Majesty to abide with us, and not to cross the river,
for then you, Sire, set yourself one against the world.
It will be said then, 'Behold, the Alexander, who

himself flees, and abandons his men to the Muscovite!
What a miserable, wretched thing of a man! Look!
Look! And the silver plate and barrels of gold that
he carried away from Saxony, he leaves to the Russ!
Ah, yes! Haha!' We poor plain-spoken subjects in
no wise can permit your Majesty to front the world
in any way by yourself, and expose your royal person
to be bespattered by the ignorant and the stupid; the
same as the Field Marshal, or Piper, or Lewenhaupt,
or any other of us. When were the unknowing taught
to know misfortune? Your Majesty desires to die: all
we old campaigners wish that; but pride – your
Majesty's pride—to offer up your pride to your
subjects, that is an offering which they could not
accept. It is given that the troops cannot cross
the river: we have neither flat-bottoms nor anchors,
nor stakes, nor piles, nor any carpenters. Therefore I ask your Majesty to remain here, and not
to throw the gauntlet down against the whole
world."

"Let the boat be made ready," was the King's
command.

Mazeppa, the chivalrous owner, had got together
his baggage, and his two tons of ducats; and sitting on
his wagon, was well over the water by now. Zaporogs
and troops of soldiers fastened their clothes on their
backs; under their arms they put boards off the
wagons, and boughs from the trees, and leapt into the
river. About midnight, the wagon of the King was
lifted on two boats lashed together. Gyllenkrook,
standing at his feet, silently handed over the map of

the farther countries drawn upon a piece of board.
No one spoke. The starry night was deep with
silence. The stroke of the guards' oars died away
over the shimmering water.

"We two will see him never again," muttered
Creutz to Lewenhaupt. "His eyes of late were
strange. There is still oil in the lamp; but I look
forward with suspense to his fortunes. How will he
encounter life as the defeated, as the derided, as an
old man?"

Lewenhaupt answered: "The cross he made for
himself has slipped down upon the shoulders of his
subjects. For all time will he remain in that marish
plain, there, lying on the forgotten graves. We
must be grateful to him for all that which he made
of us."

Through the night came the voice of Maarten
Predikare in the distance. "He has made me a by-
word of the people, and to a derision am I become.
My power is become darkened through sorrow, and
all my limbs are but as a shadow. To corruption
I have said, Thou art mine father: to the worm,
my mother and sister. And where is now my hope?
It goes down to the gates of death, when I and it
rest together in the dust."

The day dawned: and, in his bloody shirt,
Maarten Predikare rode from troop to troop, examining in the Catechism and knowledge of the
Book. The soldiery stood in silence around the
empty tent of the King. But when the cry ran
that they had to surrender, and brown-faced Bauer

the Russian General, appeared on the hill to take possession of the trophies, then Maarten Predikare came off his horse and wrung his hands. Round about sat the Cossacks upon their tired and spent horses. In front of them were laid the kettle-drums, and bugles and drums, and muskets, the thunderings of which had rolled over the battalions; and the well-known colours, which in days bygone Swedish mothers and wives had greeted in farewell, nodding from their doors, and windows, and stairways. They glanced and glittered, lying there. Non-commissioned officers, old and grim, fell on each other's necks and sobbed; some, tearing asunder their bandages, let their life's blood gutter; and two comrades, with one accord, slew each other as they were throwing down their weapons before the conquerors. Dour-faced and lowering the maimed drew past. There came young men with frost-bitten chaps, and without nose and ears; more wraiths than human men, they were. . . . There Piper, the young Ensign, hobbled by on his crutches, his feet shot through; there went Günterfelt, who had lost both hands, and in their stead, had got in France a pair of wooden ones, black and shiny; they were fingering up and down his coat. Wooden limbs clacked and creaked, and hand staves, and stretchers, and ambulance wagons.

Maarten Predikare stood there, with his hands folded. His eyes were glowing with fire. His being was violently moved within him; the old preaching spirit came upon him. He heard how the voice now faltered and grew more husky, but now became so mighty in volume, that it was to him as if he himself would be borne hence, and changed into a flame of fire. Waving toward the surrendered weapons, he addressed himself to the King's tent.

"He alone is the evil-doer. Thou mother or widow, in mourning garb, turn his picture to the wall. Forbid the children to utter his name. Thou, little Dunja, with thy playmates, wilt soon be plucking flowers on the graves of our dead; and build thy monuments up of skulls and horses' heads. Thou cripple, strike thy crutch on the hollow sounding earth, and summons him to the meeting with the thousands of victims awaiting him there, whom he did sacrifice. And yet, for all this, I know that some day we all will come before the Justice Seat, hirrupling on our wooden legs and crutches, and will say, 'Forgive him, Father, even as we forgive him, for it was our love that proved his victory as well as his destruction.'"

When no one replied, but all stood in silence and with bowed head, as if by that he was answered, his agitation grew bitter sore; and he covered his face with his hands.

"Tell me, for God's sake, tell me if he lives?" he cried.

Günterfelt took off his hat with his black wooden fingers. He replied: "His Majesty is safe."

Then Maarten Predikare bent his shaking knees. He recovered himself; and this was his stammered cry:

" Praised be the Lord of Hosts! If the King is spared, I will endure every burden which fate lays upon me."

" Yea, yea," the Swedes repeated in a murmur. 'Praised be the Lord of Hosts!" And they all slowly bared the head.

CHAPTER XIII.

BEHOLD, THESE ARE MY CHILDREN.

CORPORAL ANDERS GRAABERG stood on the Turkish waste-land, holding his field flask. Around him the fleeing Swedes and Zaporogs were passing by—many staggering about ; and on the wagons lay the wounded of Poltawa. Throughout the whole night and all that morning Anders had endured his thirst, to save the last of his water for some more neccessitous occasion ; and now his torment was become unbearable. But the instant he put the flask to his lips, he let it sink again.

" My God, my God," he stammered, " why should only I drink, when all the others thirst. Thou hast led us through the wastes, so that Thou canst now say : ' Out of your poor snow-clad fastnesses I led you, the musket on your shoulder, out into the world, so that ye might become heroes and conquerors ; yet when I searched your hearts and saw that ye had remained clean, that still ye were My children, I tore your clothes into pieces, and gave you crutches into your hands, and wooden limbs for bone, so that ye no longer should try to have power over men, but that ye might enter into My Holiness. Such power have I granted unto you.' "

Anders Graaberg remained for a little time with the flask in his hand. Then he stepped to the King, who was lying between straw sacks on his wagon, in a burning fever. He proffered him the flask. The tongue of the King clove to the roof of his mouth; his lips stuck together; they bled when he opened them. But this was his whisper :

"No! No! Give the water to the wounded. I have still one beaker full."

Right well did Anders Graaberg know that the King had none. Himself was the only one who had taken thought on the coming day, and had stored up water; for miles around them were neither wells nor pools.

But now, as he turned from the King, longing and temptation to drink once more attacked him.. He hung the flask again by his side, and went off to offer it to the wounded. He pressed his hand on its pewter top; he strove against himself; and every time he put the flask to his mouth he let it fall again, for he durst not quench his thirst. Thought he to himself: "Perchance I will be able to come at a serene mind, once I have busied myself in other things."

At mid-day, the sun burning fiercely, he noticed an old grey-haired sergeant that, almost naked, and with unbandaged wounds on his shoulders, was marching onwards with his fellows; Anders Graaberg tore his shirt into strips and bound up the wounds. But on his hand again touching the flask, his old anguish waxed anew. Thereupon he gave the staff in his hand to a wretched young baggager with feet bare

and bleeding. Yet, when after all he could not fortune to gulp down his water with a good conscience,
he grew bitter and full of ire. Swearing and sneering
he turned to Mazeppa's barrels of gold and silver.
There they rattled along on the two wagons ; and the
ill-starred soldiers were unable to buy even so much
as a dish-full of muddy water.

"Fell the horses," cried he. " Fell the horses, so
that the money barrels remain not behind us. Kill
the men too."

The soldiers did not answer him. Now he was
again showing his true nature ; formerly, in better
times, he was wont to be even as insolent and hot-
headed when marching. They observed not, that he
scarce knew what he said, before his head was down
again, and he was muttering to himself.

" Is it then wholly necessary that I must give up
the one thing of worth to me. Haha ! In that case
let us roll the barrels also into the grass there, and
touch them no more with our fingers. My God !
My God ! Once at Weperik I heard Bengt Geting,
the dying dragoon, speak with envy about the dead
that got each man of them a clean white shroud.
Mine is not so ambitious a wish ; mine is even as
lowly. Ah, I wish only not to be left behind, lying
in the wilderness, here ; I wish only to be buried in
the earth, and have the clods and green grass over me.
. . . And the few words in the lists . . .
' Anders Graaberg : fate unknown.' "

A halt was made, at the setting in of the murk, to
bury those who had died during the day ; already two

Zaporogs were shoving their spades into the earth. Among the sharp-bladed bent were a few bushes bearing cherries; and the officers and men in the meantime pulled them, and divided the fruit among themselves as a gift from the very hand of God.

Then Anders Graaberg slipped behind the bushes to drink the water unseen of the others. But just then the trumpeters began to blare, which was the token that the Muscovites were again appearing on the skyline, and visible on the far-away knolls of the parched stretches. Anders Graaberg opened his flask; but the more he breathed the dankness of the water, the more violent did his heart throb.

In the nearest wagon, dying Börje Kove, Steward of the Silver, raising himself, stared at him. Anders tried to withstand the look; but was unable; and again he thrust the life-giving liquid from him.

"Blessed are they that hunger and thirst after righteousness," said he.

As a servant of the Lord administering the sacrament, he carried the flask before him with outstretched arm, and put it to the Steward's mouth. The dying man drank the water, even to the very last drop.

Tight did Anders Graaberg hold to the side of the wagon. But when it rolled away, his hands slipped aside, and he sank in a heap among the grass.

"There is no room on the wagon for me," said he. "For all I'm but thirty years old, I'm as worn-out and tired as a man of ninety." He laid hold of one of the spades. "Yet, leave me this spade, so that I, if my strength holds, can at least open up the ground and lay me down in my last bed.   Asleep is now mine anguish.   A voice is crying in my ear: 'Behold, these are My children.' "

Anew the soldiers began their march beside the rumbling wagons, and the trumpeters turned round in the saddle.   Flights of storks hovered above the darkening wastes.   On the steppe Anders Graaberg was still kneeling, the spade in his hand.

None have ever known anything of his fate.

CHAPTER XIV.

IN COUNCIL.

In the ante-room of the Council Chamber, Secretary Schmedeman was standing with the roll of the Heads of the people in his hand; they from whom unfortunate Sweden did desire fresh guidance, and who were now about to subscribe thereto.

The nobles began to assemble. In a corner beside Falkenberg, who was ailing, Frölich, the ancient, sat with crossed arms, slumbering somewhat lightly. On a sudden he awoke.

"We must hand over the entire treasury to the King," said he.

Arvid Horn leaped to his feet with such force that his chair fell backwards to the floor. Shooting his arms into the air, he cried:

"He may keep to himself that manifestation from Heaven, and his closetings with Eva Greta; but not turn us into thieves, out of blind affection for his Majesty!"

"That is right!" Falkenberg responded, thrumming his bloodless fingers on the back of the chair. "Day after day insinuations and accusations spread among us. Not a Swede has a thought for the honour of his fellows; yet none durst say a single judicious word about him who alone caused all the blame. Ay, Horn! Do not seat yourself again! Folk are most furious against you. They think you wanted to win the same fine position by the Princess Ulrica Eleonora through the smoke of your salvoes-in-salute, as Creutz took with the thrice-blessed Princess Hedwig Sophia. Yes, yes! Speak no more about the King; read his letter instead. Read! Find you a single line there worthy of the Head of an unfortunate people?"

"Bah! Say little about the letter," answered Horn, seating himself. "Tittle-tattle for women; excuses; indifferent matter! But how can anyone wish that a man, who never bared himself in conversation, should sit him down in his tent and open out his heart on paper? But I am one with you in this: that some day he must be called to account for all this misery."

"Some day, say you!" ejaculated Falkenberg, arising all in a quiver. "Some day! Are the Swedes then become nought but cringers and flatterers! Neither Christian Thyrann nor Erik XIV. did as much evil to us as this one has; he must be of the very devil himself! Ah, since our men are all fallen on the field, the living have only the hearts of old women. And now from such must the Swedish race be propagated!"

Fabian Wrede, amicable and honourable, stood among the speakers. His voice rang out strangely mild and full of tranquillity:

"The meeting begins!" said he, turning to the open

door. " I am not one that cringes; nor was I one of those that thronged around the young King to declare him of age; and I am fallen into disgrace. The country is everything to me, is my father and mother, my home and my very memory; is all, all! I know my country bleeds to death. I know likewise that some day its doom will be uttered. But the present is not the time to spend our thoughts on that, for when God of His accord puts a crown of thorns on our heads, the greatest is not he that evades it but who presses it the closer to his head, saying, ' Father, here am I, to serve Thee.' And I tell you, that never, never, in all the past years of triumph, has our little nation been so near the true imperishable greatness as it is now."

Horn was stepping to the Council Chamber, but he turned to Falkenberg. Said he, with suppressed voice :

" My mother had other sons besides me; the bullets have found them all. Must I be worse than they ? And if one man can induce a whole nation to offer up such sacrifice, must not that man be far more than all others? "

Wrede took Falkenberg softly by the shoulder. With suppressed voice he likewise said :

" And the people, who have borne so much. . . Would you hinder these people from pressing the martyr's crown, this day, hard upon their head ? "

The nobles went into the Council Chamber, but Falkenberg, his stick supporting him, walked up and down the ante-room. At last, when he seated himself in council, the Secretary already had read aloud the long despatch. The names of the subscribers to it were being desired by him.

No man gave his name.

Falkenberg sat there, sunk deep in thought. His eyes were moist and sorrowful. All heedless of precedence, he hastily put out his hand.

" The pen. The pen," he whispered.

CHAPTER XV.

IN THE CHURCH SQUARE.

THE broad-shouldered peasant, Jöns Snare, in Mora, was eating porridge with his neighbours, Maans and Mathias. So avaricious was he, that throughout the whole winter he lay and slept in his box-bed to save light. Illumed from the skylight above, his big, flat face gleamed ill-favoured and wrinkled like to that of a hobgoblin. Slow was his speech, in a voice deep and menacing :

" I prophecy," said he, beating his hand on the wooden dish, " that the time is coming when we will chew the bark of trees. To-morrow, I kill my last cow. Every year brings fresh taxes and imposts. Now they would take the church bell, and the sacrament plate, and the corn for the poors' house."

" Ay, that's true," quoth Maans, rubbing his grey cheeks.

He put another pinch of salt into his porridge, for it was the Sabbath.

Maans also was covetous ; he went round the neighbours, counting on the salt for his porridge and the billets of wood under the kettle,

Mathias bent himself well over the table. How wrinkled and evil-faced he was, with his black teeth and snake-like eyes. Beyond all, he was the greediest of the three. Such a niggard had never existed in all the parish. So miserly was he, that he went into the sacristy to the pastor, and bade him wear wooden clogs on weekdays like to the rest of folk.

"To my simple way of thinking," said he, "God has put us, the common folk, to keep the thumb on the purse of the rich. Not a shilling will I put into the bailiff's fist!"

"But steal my nets!" Jöns Snare replied; "ye can do that!"

Quoth Maans. "Ay, that's true."

Mathias grinned, and broke the hard bread into pieces with the hammer.

"What should a man do then, when he's starving?"

Jöns Snare shook his long matted locks. He got upon his feet. His words rang so loud, that they could be heard without, before the door:

"Thou sluggard! Rather should ye take your father's old piece down from the wall, shoot the bailiff and the tax-gatherer, and hide them in the hay-stack. And before ye pipe another tune, or come to the gallows, rather should ye go to Stockholm with me, and let the fine Lords there know the peasants' mind. Peace we demand; and peace we must have!"

"That is true. Aye, we go with you!" cried Maans, standing up, his knees trembling.

Mathias likewise arose, and shook Jöns Snare by the hand. Said he:

"We begin now, then, by going to the church and speaking to the folk. We must insist on our rights."

"I'll see to it," answered Jöns Snare. "Peace there must be: we demand it."

They left the house, and, on the way, harangued to women and girls, old men and young. When they came to the square they had a following of between twenty or thirty folk.

The autumn sun shone cool and clear upon the wooded mountain heights, upon the cool sea, and the long white-washed church. In the square the peasants thronged in front of the cattle stalls, between the wagons and carts, but the penitents at Communion were not yet come out again further than the vestibule. Shaggy-haired ancients, who were come down from the forests, and already were walking about in furs, made much ado when they recognised Jöns Snare; all considered him to be the most stubborn and masterful peasant in the parish. Also the other Dalecarlians—these with the bright, open eyes, and white shirts visible between the leather breeches—turned to him. There was nothing on earth more weighty, it seemed to them, than his tardy and peevish conversation.

"Ye've been busy church-goers!" cried he to them. "That's right, ye'll learn by rote the new prayer for what is owing from subjects!"

None took time to answer him. All pressed vehemently forward. Cried they in a burst:

"The King is taken! The King is taken! The King is taken!"

"Is the King taken?" And Jöns Snare stood with tightened fists, and looked from one to the other.

"That's true!" quoth Maans.

"Be silent, thickhead, what know ye about this?" roared Jöns Snare, throwing out his clenched fists so that all fled from him.

He seated himself on the bench before the cattle stalls. But the Dalecarlians would not depart. Closer grew the ring, for none wished to lose a single word.

"Is the King taken?" he asked again.

"One tells it to another. A smith out of Falum has said that he was taken prisoner by the Pagans."

Mathias slowly crept forward. He bent himself, and stretched out his long fingers.

"What say ye, Jöns Snare about this news? I ask in all simpleness."

Jöns Snare sat with his hands on his knees, and the sunlight played upon his stiff, impassive forehead and the hard lips. He looked on the ground.

The Dalecarlians inquired, "What say ye?"

"In Stockholm, one of the Lords of Council gives his gold, another his silver plate, and the third makes suggestion that every well-to-do subject should give his riches to the Crown, and then own no more than the poor man. Only the Queen-Widow wants her income uncurtailed; she, that grab-all! And the folk in the street break the windows of Countess Piper."

"And we," cried Mathias, "we will take the musket down from the wall, says Jöns Snare."

"That is true," quoth Maans in assent.

Yet Jöns Snare continued wordless. About him all grew so silent, that nothing was to be heard save the bells.

"Ay," was his response, after a little time; and his voice sounded more bitter, deeper, and more menacing than afore. "We will take the musket off the wall, and march off as one man. By God, ye true men of Dalon, if the King is taken, then we demand that we be led against the foe to free him and help him to return."

Mathias became thoughtful. But speedily his forehead cleared, his eyes gleamed with cunning.

"To be sure, this demand is part of our old, true right!"

"That is true!" asserted Maans.

"Yea, yea, that demand is part of our old, true right," cried the Dalecarlians, raising their hands for the oath. And such a tumult and hurly-burly arose, that no longer could anyone hear the bells.

CHAPTER XVI.

THE CAPTIVES.

FAR over the desolate stretches of Smaa-land and Finnveden, there appeared strange signs and wonders in the heavens; and now since work had lost all its worth, and the coming day its every hope, the people hungered, or ate and drank riotously amid muttered maledictions. In every farmhouse a mourning mother or widow was to be found; and while she went about the duties of the day, she talked of her fallen or captured; and at night started out of her sleep thinking that she heard the rumbling of that sinister cart, the driver of which, all clad in black, took away the victims of the pestilence.

In Riddarholm Church, the body of Princess Hedwig Sophia had lain unburied for seven years, from lack of money for the necessary expenses.

There also now lay Hedwig, the aged Queen Dowager, ancestress of the King. Some drowsy women-in-waiting were keeping watch about the bier. Waxen candles were burning dim alongside the corpse, which was wrapped in a plain linen sheet.

The youngest of the women arose, yawning. She went to the window, and drawing aside the black hangings, observed if day was about to break.

Noisy footsteps rang loud from the vestibule ; and a smallish man, stiff and gnarled, trying in every possible way to lessen the noise occasioned by his wooden leg, approached the corpse. His bright, almost white hair lay thick on his head, reaching down to his shoulders.

With deep obeisance he lifted the winding-sheet. He poured an embalming preparation out of a flask into a funnel, which he introduced into the corpse. But, on the potion being somewhat slowly absorbed, he placed the flask on the matting beside the bier, and hobbled to the dame at the window.

" Is it not seven o'clock yet, Blomberg ? said she in a low voice.

" Seven has just struck. It is ill-weather outside ; I feel by the stump of my leg that a storm is brewing. Ah ! For a long time now in Sweden one cannot prophesy anything propitious. Believe me, this time also there will be just as little money for a well-ordered burial. It was but the beginning of all, when the blessed Ekerot prophesied misery and conflagrations. And after the great fire in the Castle, likewise came the fire on the island opposite. The glare of the burning Minster and Castle shone all over Upsala plain ; in Vesteraas and Lindköping, the wind blew the ashes on the cooled sites of other conflagrations. . . . And now every end and corner of the Kingdom is ablaze. My noble lady, forgive me my free speech ;

but one accomplishes more through truth than lies! That is my old saw. Once it saved my life down there by the Dnieper!"

"Saved your life! Then at that time you were Field-Surgeon, with your regiment? You must sit down beside me, and relate the story. Time passes so slowly!"

Blomberg talked in soft, respectful tones. Now and then he raised his index and middle fingers in the air, whilst keeping the others closed.

Both threw a look at the dead; there she slept in her shroud; rouged and painted with skill, her tresses finely dressed, the deepest wrinkles on her face filled in with wax. Then they seated themselves on the bench in the window-niche before the black hanging. And Blomberg, speaking low, began the tale.

"I lay senseless on the marshy field of Poltawa. My wooden leg had tripped me up, and I had got a blow from a horse's hoof. It was night when I came to myself. I felt a strange, cold hand fumbling beneath my coat. The deeds of the wicked are an abomination unto the Lord, but soft words are blessed, thought I; and without calling out I quickly seized the plunderer by the breast. From the words he stammered out in fright, I gathered he was one of those Zaporogs who had concluded an alliance with us. As a surgeon, I had attended many of them, also captive Poles and Russians; so I could make myself fairly understood in their different tongues.

"'The heart of man is vile from youth upward,' said I softly, 'But God's word will endure. No evil

Q

can befall the upright, but the godless are full of malice.'

" ' Forgive me, good sir,' the Zaporog cried in a low voice. ' The Swedish Tzar has left us wretched Zaporogs to our fate, and the Muscovite with whom we broke our word will hack, and hew, and torture, and put us to death. I would get me a Swedish coat to pass myself off as one of yourselves. Be not wrathful with me, O merciful sir.'

" To mark whether or no he had a knife, I sought for my flint and tinder while he was yet speaking ; and kindled some thistles and twigs at my feet. Immediately I observed that before me was a small, timorous old man, with a crafty, knavish face, and empty hands. Hastily leaping up like to a beast on its prey, he bent himself in the firelight over a Swed-ish ensign who lay dead on the grass within the firelight. It seemed to me that a dead man could well afford his coat to a defenceless ally, and I did nothing to hinder. But when he was drawing the garment off, a letter fell out of the dead man's pocket. I noted by the superscription that the youngster lying there, handsome and calm as though he were fallen asleep on the way home, was called Falkenberg. The letter was from his sister ; and I only read it as far as the words which have been my motto since that time : ' Ye accomplish more through truth than with lies ; ' for the next instant the Zaporog put out the fire.

" ' Are ye mad ? ' said he. 'Sir, do not draw the plunderers hither ! '

" I heeded his words but little. I repeated again and again, 'Through truth ye accomplish more than with lies.'

" ' A great phrase, old man ! And ye will see, I do as much by means of it as you with your garment !'

" ' That depends,' answered the Zaporog. ' But we must promise each other that the one who survives says a prayer for the other's soul.'

" ' That's a promise,' I cried, reaching him my hand. And I felt how I in misfortune had happed on a brother and a friend even in this barbarian.

" He helped me ; and at dawn we were marching in the long train of wounded and abandoned entering Poltawa to give themselves up. Readily they tried to hide the Zaporog among them. Huge riding boots reached up to his thighs ; the skirts of the great coat hung down to his spurs ; and as soon as any Cossack eyed him, he turned himself to one of us, and cried loud the only few Swedish words he had learned :

" ' I am a Swede, devil take me.'

" Quarters were given to my Zaporog and myself, together with eight comrades, in the garrets of a great stone-built house. We two were the first to come ; and choce for ourselves a separate little attic room, with one window to the street. There was nothing in this room save two straw mattresses. But in my pocket I had a tin flute taken at Starodub off a dead Cossack, and on it I had practisied some beautiful psalm tunes. With this I shortened away the time then. Soon we took notice that a young woman on the other side of the street came to her window as often as I made melody. Perhaps, then, I played more often than otherwise would have been agreeable to me. I do not know aright whether she was more comely and attractive than all other women ; or whether the long intermingling among men had rendered my eye less fastidious ; but on every occasion I had great enjoyment in beholding her. Notwithstanding, I never looked when she turned her face toward our window, for aye I have been embarrassed in my behaviour toward womenfolk, and never have understood correctly how to hold myself in their company ; likewise I have never sought the fellowship of men that have their heads stuffed with tales of women, and that pursue nought but amorous intrigues. Every man should keep his chastity holy, says Paul, and live not in the lusts of the heathen who know not God, so that none do wrong to his brother therein, and offer him affront, for in such the Lord is a mighty avenger.

"Nevertheless, I was of the opinion that a man ought aye conduct himself full courteous and handsome ; and because one of my coat sleeves was in tatters, I aye turned the other side to the window when I played. She was wont to cross her arms on the window-sill, and her hand, even if it was large, was rounded and white. Also she wore a scarlet bodice with silver tassels and many loopings. An old hag of a huckster, who now and then sold bread and pickles beneath her window, called her Feodosova.

"When the dark set in she lit a lamp, and as neither she nor we had shutters on the windows, we could follow her with our eyes. But I found it more decorous to turn away from the window, and recline with my Zaporog on the straw in the corner.

"In addition to my prayer book I possessed some loose pages of Muller's homilies; I read some of these and translated them to my Zaporog. When, however, I noted that he did not pay attention, I went back to things of the world again, enquiring from him about our neighbour on the other side of the street. She was not a wife, he told me. The young women of that county aye wear a long braid of hair plaited with ribbon, with a small silken knot thereon. When they are widows they wear their hair loose, as a token of mourning.

"When the dark was fallen, and we had laid ourselves down among the straw, I discovered that the Zaporog had pilfered my silver snuff spoon. But after I had got it back and reproached him for his error we slept together as friends.

"When it was day again, I was almost ashamed of myself because of my lightheartedness. Yet as soon as I had prayers with my Zaporog, and carefully cleansed and dressed myself, I was off to the window, playing one of my most select tunes.

"Feodosova was already sitting in the sunshine. So to let her see how different the Swedes be to her own people, I bade the Zaporog wash out our room; and after a few hours the whitewashed walls of it were glancing white, and without any cobwebs. All this helped to turn my attention. But straightway I sat me down again, arose my bitter thoughts that I could be so cheerful when so much pain and trouble were about me. Without, sat comrades of mine on benches and the floor of their room, making moans and speaking in whispers of their dear ones at home.

" Two of us, in turns, durst go into the open every day, and even down to the ramparts. But that night, when I laid me asleep, I was abashed to entreat of God that the lot fall on me in the coming morning. Right well knew I that if I were hankering for an hour's liberty, it was but to find some motive to go into the opposite house. And yet for all this I felt that if the turn, without my prayer for it, did in truth fall on me, I would not even then venture to go there.

" The next morning, when I went to the winaow, Feodosova lay clothed on the floor, asleep, with a pillow under her neck. It was yet early in the day, and cool; and I did not put the flute to my mouth. Meantime, while I was standing there, she must have found out in her sleep I was watching her, for she looked up, laughed, and stretched her arms; and all this so quick, that I had no leisure to withdraw myself unnoted. I reddened violently; put the flute away; and on the whole acted so awkwardly, that never have I been more discontented with myself. I fastened my waistbelt the tighter, and moved about. I took the flute off the sill, examined it, and acted as if I were blowing some dust off it. When in the end the Russian sergeant, who had the oversight of us unfortunates, explained to my Zaporog that he was one of the two allowed to go out into the town this day, I drew him into a corner and reminded him with many words not to forget to pluck me a nosegay of yellow asters which I had seen grow in the neighbourhood of the burnt houses by the ramparts. At some opportunity, then, we would present them to Feodosova, said I : she had the look of a good and worthy woman, who perhaps would send us poor devils some fruit and nuts, said I : the miserable dole of bread from the Tzar would not satisfy the hunger of any man, said I.

" He was ashamed to show himself in the sunlight out of doors. But he likewise feared to awake suspicion if he remained, so he obeyed, and went out. Hardly was he before the door than I began to rue that I had not detained him ; for, now I was all alone, my embarrassment grew the greater. I seated me on the straw in a close corner, wherein I could not be viewed ; and there I stayed.

" Despite all, the time passed not slow to me, for I had enough to think on. After awhile I heard my Zaporog's voice. Without reflecting on what I did, I went to the window. I beheld him standing with Feodosova ; in his hand a large, beautiful nosegay of asters, more recalling the flag-flower. At first she would not accept of them, saying that they were unclean things, being the gift of a pagan. He acted as if he understood her not, as if on the whole he knew but few words of her tongue ; yet, with winkings, and noddings, and gestures, he made plain to her that I had sent the flowers. In the end, she took them.

" Beside myself with rage, I went back into my

corner, and when the Zaporog returned, I seized him
by the shoulder.   Vigorously I shook him and butted
him athwart the wall.

" Nevertheless I had scarce let him go, than he was
standing again at the window in his heedless levity,
making signs to her and throwing kisses from all five
fingers.   Thereupon I came nearer, thrust him aside,
and myself made a leg.   Feodosova sat and pulled
apart the blooms, chewing the leaves and letting them
fall one by one.   My inborn courtesy prompted me :
I took courage, and began to speak before considering
how I could begin the conversation.

" ' I pray you, worthy lady, not to misinterpret the
conduct and unbecoming gestures of my companion,' I
stammered out.

" More eagerly she tugged at the flowers.

" After a time she replied :

" ' When my man was alive, he was wont to say
that, from top to toe, there were never any soldiers
so well built as the Swedes !   He had seen Swedish
captives undressed and thrashed by the women-
folk ; and how in the end the women had become so
charmed with the Swedes' good looks, that putting
their rods under their arms, they cried over the bruises.
So, to-day, I have been very inquisitive, so far : and
the fine music you play sounds so strange.'

" Now her speech by no means pleased me.   Likewise I found it not seemly to answer her in a like
fashion, as if I admired her figure and her white arms.
Instead I made a bow, took up my flute and played
my favourite Psalm, ' In my deep distress I call on

Thee.' After this we talked about many things; and although my stock of words was small, we soon understood each other so well, that no day has ever seemed shorter to me.

"At dinner time, after she had rattled for some time among the plates and bowls, she fetched out from under the roof a net, with which her husband had formerly caught fish in the river. Into this net she put a small coggie filled with steaming green kale, and a wooden flask of kvass; and the rod of the net was so long, that it could reach across the narrow street. When I drank to her health, she bowed, laughed, and said, that she thought it was no wrong to take pity on captive pagans.

"Towards evening she placed her spinning-wheel at the window, and we talked again, till darkening set in. To me it seemed nought but a sin to be so happy in the midst of our affliction, for my intentions were pure and guileless. Yet even as between the burnt and desolated dwellings by the ramparts I had seen the flag-flower gleam above the heaps of ashes, so now my heart's rejoicing seemed like unto a hymn of thanksgiving for the goodness of God to me.

"When night came on, and I had prayers with my Zaporog, and once again had caught him stealing my snuff spoon, the talkative man began to speak softly to me.

"'Well do I see, little father, you have won over dear Feodosova, and in fair truth she is as good and pure a woman as you could take to wife. That you would never engage in a love affair of any sort, I have understood from the very first moment!'

" 'Nonsense!' I answered. 'Nonsense!'

" ' Through truth one accomplishes more than with lies, you were wont to say.'

" When he combated me with my own proverb, I grew confused.

" He continued :

" ' The Tzar has promised every one of you Swedes, who becomes a subject, and embraces the True Faith, a good appointment and great reward.'

" 'You are out of your senses! But, could I take to my heels and have her with me on my horse, I would do it at once!'

" The next morning, when I had played my Psalm, I received the information, that 'twas my turn that day to go out.

" I grew ardent and restless. More careful than usual I dressed and brushed myself, borrowing, too, the ensign's coat from the Zaporog, so that I need not wear my tattered one. All the time I was deliberating : ought I to go up to her? and then what ought I to say? when in all likelihood this was the one time in my life I would be able to speak to her. How deeply would I rue it later on, in my grey old age, if I let slip this one chance from nought but embarrassment. My heart was beating more violently than ever in any affair with the enemy, myself standing with my pouch of dressings among the flying bullets and the fallen. I put the flute in my pocket and went,

" When I got into the narrow street, she was sitting at the window, and never giving an eye to me. I did not wish to ascend without having first asked her for permission, and knew not aright how I ought to set about it. And while yet considering the case, I took a couple of steps forward. Thereupon she heard me, and looked out.

" Courteously I lifted my hat. But with a wide-resounding burst of laughter she leapt up. Cried she:

" ' Haha! Look, look! He has a wooden leg!'

" I stood with my hat in my hand, and staring and staring into the air, wholly void of thought, of feeling. To me it was as if my heart had burst, and filled my breast to breaking. I believe I spluttered forth some words.

" I only yet recall that I knew not in what direction I should turn; that aye I heard her laugh; that to me everything in the world was become indifferent; that liberty in the open now called forth deep dismay to me; that all at once I was changed into a broken-hearted man.

" Vaguely I recollect a long, steep street without any paving, and a big market-place, where I was spoken to by other Swedish prisoners. Mayhap I answered them, enquired after their circumstances, and at the same time took a pull of the tobacco pipe which they offered me. I believe also that I troubled myself how long it was yet until night time, and how that I must needs return the same way, past her window, in the bright sunshine. I tried in all ways to pass the time: spoke now with this, now with that person.   But it was not long ere the Muscovite dragoons, coming along, ordered me to get home.

"As I went along the street I made up my mind not to betray myself, but to bow up to the window in some friendly fashion.   Was it her blame that so many Swedish soldiers, of whom she had expected vigour and comeliness, were now pitiful cripples, hobbling about on wooden legs?

"'Make haste there!' thundered the dragoon.   I quickened my steps, and the thud of my wooden leg echoed between the houses.

"'Kind Father in Heaven,' I murmured, 'I have served my earthly master in all uprightness, is this now the reward Thou givest me: that Thou makest me into a defenceless prisoner, whom the people pelt with dirt; into a miserable cripple, at whom the women laugh?   Yea, 'tis the reward: and Thou wilt abase me yet more, so that one day I be worthy of the Crown of Salvation.'

"When I was come beneath the window I marked that Feodosova was away from it, which was no more relief to me.   I stumbled up to my prison, and at every step I heard the thumping of my wooden limb.

"'I have spoken with Feodosova,' whispered the Zaporog.

"I gave no answer.   My luck, my blossoms grown in the ashes, lay perished on the ground, and if now they bloomed anew, I myself, full of anguish and despair, would scatter them with my wooden limb. Of what account could the whisperings of the Zaporog be to me?

" ' Ah,' he went on with, ' when you were gone out I made reproach to Feodosova, and told her that she had no idea how much you loved her, and that, were you not a stranger and heathen to boot, you would ask her to become your wife.'

" In silence I folded my hands, and bit my lips to keep my shame and affliction locked fast ; and gave thanks to God, that He, through shame and the laughter of folk, every hour abased me the more before men.

" Opening the door to the outer room, I began to talk with the others.

" ' As the wild colts in the wilderness we seek laboriously our bread. On fields which belong not to us we harvest, and store the grapes of the ungodly, and the whole night long we lay naked from lack of clothing, and without covering against the cold. The floods of rain from the mountains wash down upon us, and from lack of shelter we cling to the rocks. But we supplicate not for deliverance, O Almighty God, we only pray, " Direct us Thou, O God. Abide by us. Behold, Thou has turned Thy countenance from my folk, and put the thorn into our shoe, so that we remain Thy servants and children. In the dust of the field of battle sleep our brothers. But a more beautiful psalm of victory, than that of those conquering with the sword, Thou sayest to Thy chosen ! " '

" ' Yea, Lord, guide Thou us. Abide by us, O Lord,' repeated the prisoners in a murmur.

" Out of the darkest corner arose a voice :

" ' O that I were as in olden days when God protected me, when His lamp burnt upon my temples,
when I walked in the darkness by His light.   Yea,
even as I was in the autumn of my life, when under
my roof was fellowship with God, and my children
encompassed me about.   My heart calls out together
with Job; but no more do I hear it; and no more I
call forth, "Take Thou this trial away from me."
With mine ear have I heard speak of Thee, my God.
But now mine eye has taken witness of Thee.'

" ' Hush.   Hush,' the Zaporog whispered, and he
seized hold of me, his hands cold and trembling.
' That can be none other than the Tzar himself, coming up the street there.'

" The street was filled with men, beggars, urchins,
old women, and soldiers.

" In the midst of the throng the Tzar stepped along.
Tall and thin was he, wholly composed and without
any guard.   His only following was a swarm of jumping, yelling dwarfs.   From time to time he turned
round, and, embracing the smallest of them, kissed
him in a fatherly manner on the forehead.   He came
astand here and there in front of a house, where he
was offered a beaker of brandy, which, all in laughter,
he drained dry at one gulp.   It could be no other than
the Tzar, for instantly one was made aware by him
that he had rule over men and dominions.   He came
so near to me below my window, that I was able to
note his green headgear and brown coat with its worn
metal buttons.   On his shirt he had a large silver stud
with a sham stone ; and on his legs coarse woollen

stockings. His brown eyes sparkled and glittered. His little black moustache stood up above his lips.

" Glancing at Feodosova, he fairly went beside himself. When she came down into the street and knelt down, with a goblet in her hand, he pinched her ear, took her by the chin, and raised her head up, so that he could look into her eyes.

" ' Tell me, child,' he asked, ' can ye find me a big room where I can take bite and sup? With you, maybe?"

" On his journeying the Tzar seldom had a Master-of-Ceremonies with him, or other court official. Neither bed nor bed-linen he took with him, likewise no provisions, not even kitchen utensils or table service; but all had to be furnished in a twinkling, wherever it pleased him to take a meal. So now there was a hubbub and ado at all doors and on all steps. From one place they came with the kettles; from the other, with earthen dishes; from a third, with ladles and pot liquors. Up in Feodosova's room the floor was covered deep with straw. The Tzar himself took part in the labour, like to a common soldier; and chief control was taken by a hunched-back mannikin, that now and then set the women all at sixes and sevens, and blew his nose into the air, or contrived knavish tricks about which I cannot speak in the presence of a lady of quality.

" One time when the Tzar, with arms crossed, turned to the window, he observed me and my Zaporog, and nodded to us as one nods to a fellow companion. The Zaporog threw himself head-first on the floor, stammering out his, ' I am a Swede, devil take me ! ' But I shoved him aside with my foot, and prayed on him to get up and hold his tongue, for no Swede demeaned himself in that wise. In order, then, to protect him as much as possible, I placed myself before him, and formed front.

" ' Dat is niet übel,' said the Tzar. But immediately he went back again to his mother tongue, and asked who I was.

" ' Blomberg, surgeon in the Uppland regiment,' I replied.

" With one glance, the Tzar examined me — a glance so searching, that never have I met so all-knowing an eye.

" ' Thy regiment exists no more,' cried the Tzar, and here ye see Rehnskiöld's sword.' He drew the sword with the sheath out of his belt, and threw it down on the table, making the dishes rattle. ' But, without a doubt, you're a rogue : you're wearing the uniform of an ensign or captain.'

" I replied : ' That is a hard speech,' says John the Evangelist. ' The coat I have borrowed because my own was in tatters. Should this be thought wrong of me, I will still hope for mercy, for my proverb is worded, " With truth one accomplishes, in time, more than with lies." '

" ' Good ! Then if ye say that, take thy servant, and come over, so that we may put thy saying to the test.'

" The Zaporog shook and flinched on stepping over the way with me. But immediately we entered, the

Tzar pointed out to me a seat among the rest at the table, as if I were his equal.

" ' Seat yourself, Wooden Leg.'

" He had taken Feodosova on his knee, without thinking what was to be said against such conduct. Round about him there walked and whispered a number of boyars, now beginning to assemble.

" A dwarf, Judas by name, so called because he had a picture of that arch-villain on his necklet, took a handful of shrimps off the nearest plate, and threw them into the air, so that they fell on both men and platters. When in this wise he got the others to turn against him, he pointed to the Tzar. Making a face, he in all calm blood cried out to him :

" ' Ye do amuse yourself, Little Father ! Outside the town I had already heard folk talk of the beautiful Feodosova. But ye aye pick up the best, Little Father ! '

" ' Ye do that,' cried the other mannikins round about. ' Ye're a true-born thief, Peter Alexievitich.'

" Now and then the Tzar gave a laugh and answered them. Yet for the most he sat full earnest and thoughtful, his eyes moving like two glittering insects in the sunshine.

" There came into my mind how that once I had witnessed Karl XI., of blessed memory, in conversation with Rudbeck, and how at the time it had seemed to me that Rudbeck, for all his many becks and bows, stood far higher in importance than the King. Here it was the contrary. For although the very Tzar went about, and worked, and let himself be treated worse

than a knave, yet for all this I perceived but him alone
. . . and Feodosova. In the most trifling things,
I descried his mind.

"That buzzed in my brain: and humbly, among
the straw, I bowed my knee.

"'Your Majesty,' I stammered, 'To speak the truth
is less dangerous than to lie. Therefore I supplicate
of you to let me drink of some liquor yet once more,
for my worthy master, who is as like as well as unlike your Majesty, has accustomed me these last few
years to drink of nought but filtered marsh water.

"Hereupon the right cheek of the Tzar started
atwitching,

"'Yes, by St. Andrew,' said he; 'I am unlike my
brother Charles. He hates women like a woman; and
squanders the wealth of his folk as a woman does the
wealth of her husband; and slanders me like a woman.
But I honour him as a man. To his health, Wooden
Leg. Drink! Drink!'

"The Tzar sprang to me, took me by the hair and
held the goblet to my mouth; the Astrakan beer ran
down my chin and neck. At each health two soldiers
in yellow and brown uniforms with blue collars
entered and let off their pistols, so that the stuffy
room, already filled with tobacco smoke and the stink
of garlic, grew thick with gunpowder smoke.

"Once more the Tzar seated himself at the table.
Throughout the hubbub he would remain seated,
thinking; but never did he allow the others to cease
toasting and become as serious as himself. Again he
drew Feodosova on his knee. Poor, poor Feodosova!

There she sat, drawn together a little ; her arms hanging down, and mouth somewhat open, an she were expecting blows and thrashings in the midst of all his caressings. Thus it was she had not the courage to snatch the sword off the table, press her artery against its sharp edge, and so save her honour ere it was too late. What mattered it that she had made sport of my wooden leg and misfortune. Oh! I would that it were only granted me to preserve her honour with my life. Never aforetime had I been so near her, and never had I seen so clearly how wonderfully beautiful she had been made by the hands of the Creator. Poor, poor Feodosova! If only you had known in your heart that pure intent with which one friend viewed thee in thy abasement, and offered prayer for thy well-being !

"The orgy lasted hour after hour. The most licentious of the boyars and dwarfs already lay on the straw, or retched, and made water. But the Tzar, himself, aye just arose and leant out over the window.

"'Drink, Wooden Leg, drink,' he ordered, and hunted me round the room with a bumper in his hand, and bade the boyars hold me till I emptied it. The twitching on his face aye got the more gruesome to view.

"When in the end we sat again at the board, he filled three earthern bowls to the brim, and set them before me.

"'Now, Wooden Leg,' said he, 'must ye drink enow of these, and explain the import of thy saw.'

" I got up, as well as I could.

" ' Thy health, O Tzar,' cried I. ' For truly thou art born to command.'

" ' Wherefore,' asked he, 'should the soldiers present arms and salute me, if there were any others more worthy to rule ?   What in the world is more useless than an unserviceable prince?   The day I find my own son not worthy to inherit my great and beloved dominion, the same day he must die.   Thy first truth, Wooden Leg, needs no toasting ! '   And the pistols cracked, and all drank save the Tzar.

" Then I gathered the rest of my understanding together, even as a miser his coins, for I thought that if I could talk soft and smooth to the Tzar, maybe my Feodosova might be saved.

" ' Yea, indeed, your Majesty,' I continued, taking up one of the bowls.   ' This is Astrakan beer, brewed of mead and brandy, with pepper and tobacco in it. Strong does it burn the throat before it refreshes one; and when it does refresh one, it makes him drowsy.' With this I threw the bowl on the floor, so that it broke into a thousand atoms.

" Then I took up the second one.

" ' This is wine of Hungary.   " No longer drink water," says the Apostle Paul to Timotheus, " but take a little wine for thy stomach's sake, and because thou art oft-times ailing."   So says a holy man to one a weakling and stay-at-home.   But go ye out on the battlefield, among the freezing and the pain-stricken, and, tell me, could this bowl of sweet wine be passed round the many unfortunate, parched ones, to slaken thirst and ease qualms of death ? ' With this, like-wise, throwing the bowl on the floor, I broke it into pieces.

" At last I took up the third one.

" ' This is brandy. It is treasured little by the rich and fortunate, for with them it is not thirst which longs for gratification, as the beast of burden longs for the spring ; with them they but wish something wherewith to increase pleasure. But brandy is all potent the very moment it passes over the tongue, even as an autocrat is, the very instant he steps over the threshold ; and a few drops of it also brings ease to the dying and those lying bleeding. Therefore I term brandy the best of drinks, for I am speaking as an old campaigner. And through truth one accomplishes more than with lies.'

" ' That is right! That is right!' the Tzar shouted lustily, accepting the toast ; and he drank while the pistols crashed. Then he gave me two gold pieces. ' You must have a pass and a horse ; and, aye where-ever you go, you must tell of Poltawa ! '

" Then once more I knelt down in the straw and stammered :

" ' Your Majesty . . . in my humbleness and simplicity. . . . There sits a . . . a good and pure woman.'

" ' Haha ! ' yelled the boyars and dwarfs, trying, all astagger, to rise to their feet.

" The Tzar got up, and led Feodosova to me.

" ' I understand. Even he that hobbles along with a wooden leg can fall in love ! Good. I present her to

thee, as she is and stands; and ye must have a good
post with me. I have promised that every Swede
who enters our service, and goes over to our faith, he
should be one of us.'

"Feodosova stood like one asleep, and stretched
out her hand to me. She had laughed at me? What
about that! I had forgotten it! She would soon
have paid no more attention to my wooden limb, for
I would have taken care of her, and worked for her,
and made a comfortable home for her. I would have
taken her into my arms like to a child, and asked her
if a true and upright heart could not bring another to
surrender. Mayhap she already had her answer on
her lips; for now her whole demeanour was greatly
radiant, and grew warm to me; and her countenance
cleared.

"Far away, in the corner house at Prastgatan,
in Stockholm, sat an old and lonely woman with her
book of sermons, giving ear, full of expectation that
a letter would be left at her door, or an invalid enter
with greetings from remote lands—one whom she
could ask whether never again would I return, or was I
already under the sod. For her, I had put up a prayer
every night. In the tumult of battle, amongst the
stretchers and the moaning wounded, I had thought of
her. But at this hour I had now no more mind of her.

"I saw and comprehended nought else but Feodosova. Yet, despite all, I was struggling within me;
I thrilled with some weighty significance which was
for ever pressing on my heart. I did not apprehend it.
Only little by little I could make it clear to myself.

" I bent over Feodosova, to kiss her hand But
she whispered :

" ' The Tzar's hand ! The Tzar's hand ! '

" Then did I bend over to him, and kissed his hand.

" ' To my faith,' I murmured very slow, ' and to my
Royal Master I must not be untrue.'

" The Tzar's cheek twitched more violently, and the
dwarfs in their fright dragged the Zaporog out ot his
corner. The Tzar himself made merry over the
comical figure of him, and laughed. But his arm
began to move in convulsive spasms. His face
became ashen-grey. His body shivered with one of
his dreadful nervous attacks. He stepped to the
Zaporog, and dealt a blow with his clenched fist; the
blood gouted from the man's nose and mouth.

" In a voice of fury, and so changed that one could
scarce have known it again, the Tzar roared :

" ' You liar ! I have seen through ye, since first
you came into the room. You are a Zaporog ; a rebel
concealed in Swedish clothing. . . . On the wheel
with him ! . . . On the wheel with him ! '

" All, even to the tipsy, commenced to tremble, and
pressed to the door.

" One of the boyars in his terror let cry :

" ' Put forward the woman ! Shove her on ! As
soon as he sees the comely faces and bodies of women-
folk, he'll be quiet again.'

" They seized Feodosova, and tore her bodice open
over her bosom. Sobbing softly, she was thrust step
by step to the Tzar.

" All became dark before my eyes. Going backward,

I staggered out of the room. Under the stars I remained standing in the street, and heard how the din died down and the dwarfs began to sing.

"Then I folded my hands and brought to mind that promise made upon the field, to pray for the soul of the poor sinner. But the more I spake to God inwardly, anew my thoughts went astray. My prayer became a supplication for one, a greater sinner : for him who, with his last faithful followers, was wandering about on desolate steppes. . . ."

.   .   .   .   .

With a troubled glance at the coffin, the surgeon became silent. Then the lady and he approached the catafalque.

"Amen," said she. And both again spread the covering over the waxen white Queen Dowager, mother of the Charleses.